Keep
in
Touch

I hope you enjoy reading
it as much as I enjoyed
Writing it!

Adeline Hamble

Adeline Hamble

ACKNOWLEDGMENTS

Thank you to all those who cheered me on along the way. My family and friends are amazing. I'm grateful for their encouragement, support, and love.

My husband Aaron tells me every day to live my dreams. I have my very own love story with him, and I can't believe my luck.

My children, who are the reason I breathe air, give me the strength to do hard things. Without them, I would be lost.

Erin, who has always been my biggest cheerleader, thank you. I admire the joy you find in others' accomplishments. You make me a better human and I love you.

Michelle, my first friend in this life and first editor, who spent countless hours pushing me to be my best, and schooling me on the ways of the Brits, I love you. Thank you.

Amanda, who has walked hundreds of miles with me as I drone on about this project, and then took time to help edit, thank you.

To all my romance-loving friends out there; Kate, Stacy, Lexie, and Shelly, who endured the copies they had to comb through a few times, thank you. I'm surrounded by some kick-ass women, including my cul-de-sac of smut loving moms and wives. Great minds think alike, and my village is certainly like-minded.

To all those that read Mel's story, Thank You!

Prologue

My best friend has gone completely insane and I'm loving it. Mel informed me that she has accepted a new position in London, and I'm dragging her to coffee immediately. It's a six-month contract and she will need an analytics specialist. I need to make sure I'm her first pick for the project and have her swear in blood this isn't a joke. The past few years have not been the best for me and my son Jack. Mel isn't exactly loving life either.

The elevator opened to her floor and I was reassured to find her waiting to get on and head down. "Rita, I told you that I would meet you there," Mel muttered, raising her hands to her hips and stepping in.

"Well let's use this as an example proving you are always good to your word, yes? You say it and you do it. Understood?" I smirked.

"Coming on pretty strong with the guilt for nine in the morning," Mel said linking her arm in mine. "I've already talked with Eva and whatever family would care. We are going. That is if you are still interested."

Eva is Mel's seven-year-old daughter. We are both single moms. Her husband died before we became friends, and my son's dad was either in California pursuing acting...or recently married to a Wiccan in Idaho. I own my mistakes – I'm just not sure which mistake created Jack.

The crowded elevator opened and we all poured into the busy street. It was a hot day even though summer was coming to an end. "Hell yes I'm interested," I said as we walked towards the aroma of coffee.

Mel sashayed into the shop first and motioned for me to sit in a booth while she ordered. She looked extra gorgeous today. She had long dark hair, great skin, and an athletic body. For someone so ridiculously smart - she had a hard time seeing these amazing qualities in herself.

That girl was always questioning her own decisions and self-worth. The choice to leave America for a six-month project was the right one and I had to help her see that. We both needed a fresh start. *I wonder how much Paul had to do with this.*

She came over with two iced coffees and her typical warm smile. "I'm not backing out," she insisted. "I won't know anyone there but you and Paul so I'm relieved you are going."

"And there it is," I quipped. "The elusive Paul. Are you staying with him? Did he talk you into this?"

Mel instantly blushed. Paul and Mel were pen pals. I had been friends with Mel for a while before she revealed her relationship with him. He wasn't an acquaintance or a casual buddy you catch up with, but a deep friendship that meant something to her. He was from the United Kingdom and they got set up with some letter writing thing in elementary school. Mel follows through with everything so decades later they are still at it.

"Rita! He's married," Mel exclaimed.

"So, no then?" I asked.

"No, I'm not staying with him, and no he didn't talk me into it. He's definitely for it. I think I've dropped enough hints that I'm miserable here, and I just didn't have the courage to go through with moving until now. He's supportive."

"Whatever gets us across the pond. I can't survive another Maine winter. Plus - I always saw myself with a British guy."

Mel threw her head back and laughed. "Insufferable!" she giggled.

"Anyway, it's going to be great," I said. "Lynn is over there too. You have met her once or twice. She runs some type of tech support team. I'll ask her for some housing recommendations."

Mel's red hue returned. "Actually, I'm going to write to Paul and have him set us up. I have my contract and yours so I know the cost of living and all that. His family handles property so who better, right?"

"Whatever gets me over there, I guess. We could also just email him. Just a thought but what do I know?"

She brushed me off and sipped her coffee before responding. "I have the letter ready because I knew you would accept. I'll send it today and he always gets it under a week. He'll have a month to set us up. Plenty of time."

The fact that she was depending on Paul to take care of us and she was blushing every time we said his name was not lost on me. Mel wouldn't admit she was in love with Paul, but her actions told a different story. I always thought she insisted on writing so she could keep him at arm's length. Never too close.

"If you have faith in him then I do too. I'll head upstairs to sign the contract as soon as we are done here," I asserted. "We are doing this together – you and me." We brought our cups together in a toast and smiled.

She had been through so much heartbreak – this was her chance to be happy.

This was my chance to bring them together.

CHAPTER 1

Dear Paul,

I hope this letter finds you well. I could ask about your daughter's recital and your wife's birthday - both of which I truly hope were just super - but the truth is I need to rant about myself for the next 3 pages.

Prepare for a nonstop droll of my latest life decision in which I will be taking you up on your offer. You know, the one you gave me six years ago. Something to the tune of - if you ever need anything, anything at all.

I was supposed to let you know if you could help me in any way. I get people make all sorts of promises to recent widows, but being as all our correspondence is on white paper, your promise reads more like a contract.

I don't plan on forcing you into a corner here, but I've decided I need to leave Maine. Lord, I know what you are thinking as you read this - I know I know I KNOW. Long time overdue. You win. And if you so choose to write back a giant, I TOLD YOU SO on the first page, you are already forgiven.

The thing is, I really thought there was a piece of him still here and I've been wallowing in it for some time now. It gave me comfort at one point, but the last few months have made me realize that I'm living on a carousel from hell that I can't get off.

Not to mention I'm the only one of my friends in the prime of our mid-thirties no longer getting off -period.

Same crap over and over, and I've realized that this Groundhog Day never ends. If you don't know what Groundhog Day is because London may have missed the mid-nineties Bill Murray experience, please stream it now. It's a true treasure and gives a wonderful representation of the current purgatory I'm going through.

What brought this decision about? Well, it wasn't you, although refer to my previous paragraph where you are more than welcome to still write the - I told you so. It was the July 4th party last month at my Uncle's house. July 4th you better know about, Londoner. That's your history too, and probably the source of why most Americans think tea is dumb.

So, I'm having a drink, maybe four. Whatever, this widow gets a pass and an Uber when my daughter is having a sleepover there.

My cousins are all somehow in their twenties because I'm old and they are drinking as well. Every damn one of them in a relationship or engaged. So, problem number one - I'm alone and quickly realize I'm the only one alone. My giant Catholic family and no one else is single. Complete bullshit.

Problem number two - I bring this up to them and discuss that I haven't dated anyone since Mitch passed away and none of them know what I'm talking about.

"Who is Mitch?" some chick named Ever slurs out of her hard lemonade. Who the crap names their kid Ever? Why is my cousin dating an idiot?

All good questions, right? Anyway!

So, I walk (stumble) up to the kitchen in which - I repeat this horrible story to my Uncle. It takes him like five minutes to register what I'm talking about. I may have been slurring too, but the point is, he had forgotten Mitch for five minutes.

I go apeshit and he gives me a big lecture about living in the past. He said all this crap about others moving on, and they never met him, and I need to calm down. I get an Uber and leave in a huff.

Then the Uber driver - who I repeat all this to - AGREES with my damn Uncle.

I figured I would just shake it off and avoid my family at our next function like the passive-aggressive maniac I am, but then Monday I got the offer for the Prometheus deal again. I mean, they won't give up, right? Except for this time, I accepted in my fury.

I told Eva about it thinking she would completely freak out, but she's probably the most mature seven-year-old on the planet and now thinks living in London for six months will make her a princess by association. Using her to back out is now kaput and I guess it's happening.

This is where you need to read above about your promise. It's above the - I told you so part.

I need a condo or duplex or cottage or whatever the hell you live in over there that's close enough to the tube or subway or whatever the hell you call public transportation.

Also, Rita is coming. I know I talk about her like she's a wild banshee of a woman but she's also a true friend. I need her right now, and she wouldn't go unless I did. Her son is coming too. It will be good for both of us to have familiar faces when I realize I have made a horrific mistake.

It will also be helpful to have someone force me on the plane and off the plane and into the office the first day while I'm trying to claw my way out of the country. Rita will be excellent at that.

She can live near me but not with me. That is why I'm begging you to find me a place so I can be settled before I'm forced to let her takeover. I love her dearly, but I can't do the roommate thing. I've enclosed the contract with what my company is paying for room, board, food, and childcare.

I also need a nanny person. Isn't England full of those? I don't need her falling out of the sky with an umbrella, but if you or your wife could put out some feelers, I would appreciate it. Rita and I could share someone because the kids are the same age.

We leave in a month. I'm putting in writing that this absolves you of your contractual promise. Widow's honor.

Please don't set me up above a pub or male review no matter how much you may think I need to get out there. I'm moving to England for six months. I'm out there.

~~Hearts and Stars~~

Mel

P.S. I really do hope Nina's recital was perfect. I know she was nervous. Also, I hope your wife was genuinely surprised by her party, but God only knows. Women are experts at faking everything from orgasms to shock so it's a crapshoot whether or not she had a clue.

CHAPTER 2

Eva is asleep in the van with her head drooping in that way parents think will most definitely break their kid's neck. How is that comfortable? I reach back to try and tip her into a more reasonable position without waking her. A fool's errand.

"I think it's great that we are across the street from each other." Rita is beaming in the far back of the van staring out the window like a child. "The kids can have sleepovers. And you know if one of us has a good night out - it could be helpful."

I can't figure out if she thinks England is a fresh start or a husband hunt. She already met a guy on the plane. The idea of dating at all makes my heart race and stomach churn.

I continue to gently tap on Eva's head. "I think you need to focus on work and this giant project we have to pull off in just under six months."

Our company names all our new startups after Greek Gods. Not shocking our board is ninety percent male. Prometheus is supposed to be the new wave of marketing. A way to give tools to individuals and small businesses so they can have more precise advertising. It's not the gift of fire, but we think highly of ourselves.

"Lighten up buttercup." Rita turns her head from the window and smirks. "If you think I'm not over here to get some action - you're crazy."

Rita never knew the father of her son Jack. Well, she knew him for a few hours. Jack has reached an age of questions and that woman does not have the answers. This trip is hope for distraction, or to buy her some time. Jack is sleeping soundly on Rita's lap with a blanket pulled over his head. I imagine he's used to drowning her out.

Eva finally rests her head on the side of her seat. It slips under her seatbelt ever so slightly, but I accept it as a win. Her blonde curls cover her face and wisp around her as she breaths out. We are almost there anyway.

I huff as I turn around in my seat and become slightly startled. I keep forgetting the side of the road is opposite and I press on an invisible brake on the empty floor. "Did you send Paul a Thank You for finding us our places?"

"Yes," Rita said turning back to the window. "And I sent it via email like a human living in the twenty-first century. He then responded no problem in like half a minute - because it's email."

Paul and I have been writing paper letters for about twenty-five years. There are shoeboxes stacked full of them back in Maine. Rita doesn't get it. Maybe I don't get it, but something is comforting in the process.

In the nineties, before computers and email became the norm in every household, we were part of the Letters Abroad grade school program. Some years we sent letters every week and some years I maybe got two, but it never stopped. When Mitch died, Paul sent me a letter every day for a month until I responded with a page that said *That'll do pig*.

"Well, we don't work like that." I suddenly felt a flutter in my stomach that I would soon meet Paul. I haven't seen a picture of him since high school. We kept missing our chance.

His wife wasn't a fan of social media. Our spouses were okay with our friendship, but we never talked on the phone or did video chat. That felt like crossing a line. "I think he'll appreciate my gratitude in person more than email after all this time."

Rita let out a hoot. "I know what he may appreciate. You two have one hell of a foreplay story."

The driver cleared his throat uncomfortably, making his presence known. I took the hint.

"Seriously, you are only here for six months. You need to make the most of it and have him forget that controlling wife of his," Rita continued - obviously not getting the hint.

I mouthed I'm sorry to the driver who couldn't hide his smile.

The next twenty minutes was silent, and I was grateful. The kids slept and I let my mind relax. My anxiety was high from the lack of sleep and long flight. I refused to have a drink or even melatonin. Nerves had gotten the better of me and I had to be aware of my surroundings. I was a single mom entering a foreign country.

I closed my eyes and pictured the best possible end to my day. I would walk into a beautiful home. Eva would be jumping with delight behind me. My bags would still be neatly packed as if TSA hadn't destroyed them and rifled through my panties. The fridge would magically have wine and dinner.

My therapist had been working with me on what she called positive cognitions. I mean, there's not a chance in hell my fridge has more than an open box of baking soda, but the thoughts help. The sleepless nights and panic attacks are still there, but the more I try to picture the best next hour, afternoon, or day, the less they occur.

The van weaved in and out of narrow roads with ease. I saw houses lined up, two together with small walkways in between. Paul had used the phrase semi-detached homes, and I had no clue what he was talking about. I saw some pictures of the interior and I trusted him.

These were duplexes and triplexes. Two or three families in a larger home sharing a wall or two. I was grateful that Rita was across the street and not on the other side of a wall. I then felt bad for her neighbor considering her plans for nightly activities.

All the yards were neatly manicured with flower boxes in the windows. The homes were pale shades of white and tan, but the doors were all different. Some bright red or others a butter yellow.

The car slowed and gently parked on the street in front of a light blue door of a duplex. "This is 42 Winlin Ave," the driver said tipping his head to me. "Right there is 65 Winlin," he pointed. "The one with the burgundy door. I'll help you with your bags."

Rita began crawling through the middle of the van and Jack's head thumped on the seat. It's a blessing God granted her with a boy. You have to be tough with Rita as a mother.

"That's me - 65 Winlin, and I'm not waiting," she squealed. She about plowed the driver over opening her door and he scrambled with her luggage.

I already had the keys in my hand. They were heavy and brass-colored. They looked like they belonged on a desk in my grandmother's house. There was something very British about them.

I had made it all the way here. Only a few more steps. I turned back to see Eva's chest rising and falling in her seat. In the distance, Rita was shuffling quickly with heavy bags, and our driver was trying to unload the back of the van to catch up with her. Jack was still out curled up under his blanket.

I stepped out and started towards the blue door. Matching flower boxes lined both windows. The vinyl was older but freshly painted. Paul had done a good job.

I'll just peek in and make sure it's somewhat in order before carrying Eva to her room.

The key fit the lock and clicked open. I pushed in reminding myself of the positive thoughts from the car ride.

A step forward and I was then pulled forward, my hand clutching the doorknob that just got yanked from the other side. I flung my other arm like a baby bird trying to balance myself. I fell to my knees and then finally got the good sense to let go of the door.

"What the hell," I stammered looking back up.

There stood a man who didn't seem the least bit sorry for flinging me off balance. He had a pained expression on his face like I had pushed him.

"Sorry," I said. *Dammit, why do women always apologize?*

I got to my feet, and still no words from him. He was much taller than me, maybe 6' 3", and dressed in faded jeans and a white shirt. He had dark hair that was longer but didn't look unkempt. An awkward pause passed between us, and then I tried to reach out my hand as he brushed by me to exit. *Okay, maybe we don't shake hands in this country.*

"I said I'm sorry," I shot at him again, brushing my hands off on my jeans. Still an apology - but one with attitude.

He didn't turn or slow his pace. His broad back straightened and he ran his hand through his hair - visibly agitated at either my apologies or my presence.

"Look at that fine piece of ass." Rita had returned and walked around the side of the car. I was too busy fuming in his direction to notice.

"More like an asshole," I said turning back to the duplex. The door was still open, and I was disappointed to see two interior front doors. I share an entire middle wall with this jerk instead of apartment-style - on top of each other.

Rita's arms flung around me. "Don't start off negative. Americans are sensitive."

I feigned a smile as I turned towards her to hug her. As I pulled away, I saw him a little further down the street.

Facing us.

Facing me.

Staring.

I took a step away from Rita towards the street, and he quickly turned and left. Resuming his pace, I could see his back muscles tense again through his fitted shirt. This guy does not want a neighbor Mel, that's all.

I crossed my arms and watched him leave. I hated to admit it, but he was handsome, so watching him walk off wasn't exactly a chore. When he reached the corner he turned back, glanced back for a moment, then lowered his head as he left.

CHAPTER 3

I'm sending this letter to your new home, which I hope is working out well. I would love to come and see it soon, but unfortunately, Nina is feeling poor.

She was starting on a fever when you left, and it's now become quite the illness. I would hate for darling Eva to succumb, so we will be forced to stay away until everyone is on the mend.

The nanny hunt has been more difficult than I thought. The area you are staying in doesn't have many childcare centers, but it was close to the exchange school and your office, so I thought it was the best option.

There is an older woman who lives at the end of the street. Her name is Mrs. Jane MacArthur, and she's nearing eighty. Now, from personal experience, a seven-year-old needs no more than a snack and an iPad - so you don't need anyone spry.

As you never take my advice unless you feel you have come up with the idea on your own, I leave it to you to decide. I've included Mrs. MacArthur's telephone.

She insists she's more interested in the company and wouldn't want to charge very much. That would leave some room in your budget.

I suggest you utilize that windfall and head to the local bar at the end of your street. It's called Winlin Wag. We sometimes get so smashed that it's helpful to have the name of your street on the place in case you forget where you are.

In all seriousness, please meet some neighbors. I would feel better if you made some friends here. What if you love England and stay forever?

I suggest you take the few days you have before you start work to make a trek downtown. The tube system can be a bit dodgy if you haven't used it before. I know how anxious you can get and feeling confident about arriving on time and safely your first day is worth the trip.

Best ~~ Paul

P.S. Nina did great at her recital. Unsure if my Claudia was surprised at her party, but she was surprised at the bill. All worth it, I say.

P.P.S. Maybe leave behind Rita and get dinner by yourself at the Wag. She seems to be someone who would steal the show. I'm sure she's lovely. Just my two cents.

CHAPTER 4

I spent far too long walking from room to room like a zombie trying to soak up my surroundings. Paul's letter had been on the table with other welcome mail, and it jolted me out of my daydream. No postmark. Had he been here?

It took Rita maybe an hour to throw herself into her new home. I had barely arranged our luggage in the bedrooms as she plopped on my couch announcing she was ready to go out on the town. The guy she had met on the plane asked her for a drink already.

Sensing my terror, she promised that Lynn and her husband were going as well. They also worked for our company and had been living in England for over a year now. I couldn't remember meeting them before, but Rita made friends with everyone. They were all too ready to show her the sights.

I bowed out and she didn't seem surprised or disappointed. Eva and Rita walked back to her house hand in hand so I could unpack and get myself sorted. I would take over kid duties for her date later.

The house was fully furnished and wasn't too far off from my style. It was bright and airy with lots of light. The furniture was smaller to accommodate the tighter living quarters.

There was a tan couch facing a television. An oversized white chair in the corner with a tall lamp that would be perfect for reading. Only a few pieces of art, painted flowers, and landscapes hung on the wall.

I took a glance at myself in the mirror by the front door. My thick dark hair was a mess of knots that I would have to deal with later. For now, up in a ponytail it went. My blue eyes seemed bloodshot and sunken. I seemed to have avoided a massive stress breakout, but there was still time for disaster before my first day.

My stomach growled. When did I eat last? Did I eat today? What is today?

I pulled out my phone. No messages, but no huge shock there. It was after two in the afternoon here which meant it was morning back home. I didn't eat lunch or dinner last night. My credit card was already switched to accept foreign transactions and I had some cash. The point being, I had the power to feed myself. I texted Rita.

> *Hey I know you are eating later but I'm dying. Hungry?*

Typing dots. No dots. Typing dots. Jesus woman.

> *I shouldn't - need to fit in this tight dress.*
>
> *Okay well I'm going out. Is Eva hungry?*
>
> *She ate like 3 donuts when we landed. She's fine.*

Ask her please

Typing dots. No dots. Typing dots.

She said she isn't hungry but will be hungry later. She's like a philosopher.

haha I'll text you before I leave the shop just in case.

Don't tempt me devil woman. TIGHT DRESS

I took a quick shower using extra conditioner to comb out my mane with minimal tears. The hot water felt amazing even though I was using the smallest and maybe oldest shower known in operation. I was just amazed I had a bathroom separate from Eva. Another point to Paul.

I managed to find my favorite pair of jeans packed away, soft and worn in a way that made me feel confident and comfortable. I grabbed a tank top and slides and felt almost human again. My hair was still a little damp, but at least I was clean for the public.

Throwing it back up in a ponytail, the front hall mirror shook with the slam of a door. Then the sound of footsteps clear as a bell - and the toss of keys.

Shit you can hear everything. Maybe it's just because I'm right by the front entrance. Whatever, I'm leaving.

Heading out the door I still had some bitterness from our morning encounter. I couldn't stand people like him. People that felt they owed no kindness to anyone else. Kindness gets people through the most tragic and horrible things in life and death. I would know. It costs nothing and gives everything. Who does he think he is?

I pulled the front door wide open, jumped, and slammed it behind me as fast and hard as I could. The table in the foyer jumped so I was sure it got his attention.

Smirking I almost skipped to the street. I could see Eva and Jack's heads on the other side of the sofa in Rita's window. We were here and safe and that was all that mattered. Their kindness was what mattered.

I turned back to my new home and - oh shit - I didn't deserve what was looking at me. *Well maybe I did a little, but he acted like an immature ass first.*

He was standing in his window holding the curtain. I swear I could almost see the vein throbbing in his neck. His eyes were narrowed, and his jaw was clenched. His stare was unnerving and gave me a chill.

I crossed my arms in defiance and thought about giving him the bird. Before I got the nerve, he put his face in his hand and threw the curtain back.

I have six months of this to look forward to. It had been less than two hours and we seemed to already hate each other. Just great.

CHAPTER 5

Dear Carmela,

14th December 2003

I've been thinking a lot about your last letter. I'm responding 4 days after I received it, but it kept me up every night. I get that we are young and crazy things happen. I'll admit I have not been the best boyfriend in my past relationships either. I've also had some parties (I assume that's what a "kegger" is) where things got out of hand.

One night – my mates and I ripped apart my fence for firewood after a bottle of whiskey. My mum found us passed out with a smoldering back lawn and hands full of splinters. Point being – we all make dumb mistakes when smashed. Some things, like this, are unforgivable.

What you said to him - the skirt you wore - a guy you talked to –

I don't give a fuck if you walked in – ignored him – took your top off and lap danced your ex in front of him – then had a fag and put the butt out on his face.

He does not hit you.

You could hate his dog – wreck his car – shag his brother.

He does not hit you.

There is NOTHING in this world you could do to provoke it or accept it.

Don't you ever see him again. You tell your mum today. I don't care if you have to show her this letter to break the ice. You hand it to her and highlight the part where Carmela Morgan went to a party with her boyfriend and it ended with her eye swollen shut because he's a cunt bastard.

I'll somehow find money, a passport, and a flight to America if I don't get a letter back that you have ended it. He's not sorry – he's a wanker.

He'll do it again. There isn't a chance he will. There isn't a chance he won't. If a man hits you once it's happening again.

Stand up, find your mum, and tell her. Now Mel – I love you.

Paul

P.S. I do love you. You can do this.

CHAPTER 6

The bar wasn't what I had planned, but I had no idea where a grocery was, and my stomach was in knots. I was technically taking Paul's advice even though it was kind of by default.

I wish I had a pen and paper right now. I could write to him while I ate. Eating alone was never really my thing. Mitch and I had been on and off since high school, so it never really grew on me. I needed to get my bearings in this town. Also, I need to figure out the tube thing.

Dammit, I wish I had some paper.

I sat at the bar to seem less pathetic. The bartender shot me a kind smile as she walked my way. She looked to be around my age. She had on jeans and a T-shirt that said Winlin 10K Classic. Her nametag read Trish.

"What'll it be? A pint?" she chirped.

"Um whatever the crowd likes best on draft I guess," I said, not seeing any menus around.

"Well the local preference is Guinness, but it's a bit bold."

"I like bold and dark beer. Sounds perfect. Any food recommendations? I bet fish and chips is a bit on the nose."

She gave me a chuckle pouring my pint. "It's good here, I will say. We don't get many Americans so I'm not sure it will be to your tastes. I'll bring you a child's portion and if you don't like them no harm no pay, okay love."

"Thanks," I replied, thankful for a kind greeting in this country. She works for tips, but it still counts. "My name's Carmela. Everyone calls me Mel."

She set my beer on the counter as she hollered an order towards the back wall. "I'm Patricia, but if you call me that I'll be ill. Call me Trish. You came in on foot. Are you staying around here?"

She was perceptive. I could tell already there was a small-town vibe to this place. I need to be careful that I don't piss off anyone else. *He did have it coming though.*

I took a generous sip of my beer before responding, "Yes, well I guess I live here now for at least six months. I'm working abroad and I don't have a car. Not that I would be comfortable driving here yet."

"Most people don't drive around here," she said. "You will fit right in. So, are you staying in the Winlin houses?"

I nodded before taking another swig. With no food in my belly, I could already feel the warmth and relaxation washing over me. Good thing I was walking.

"Me too," Trish said. "Lots of these folks do, I guess. They are older but kept up well by the owners. It's safe here. You'll like it."

"Do you run? I mean, your shirt is all. Are you a runner?" *Lord, I'm awkward.*

A customer at the bar lifted his finger asking for another and she started on his pint. "I do, but mostly so I can eat. You look fit. Is it from running?"

I blushed at her compliment. I never thought of myself as someone with an envious figure. Mitch would always go on and on about how he loved my body. I think I swayed twenty to thirty pounds back and forth when we were together, but he always made me feel beautiful. "I run," I said. "But it's been a while. I would like to get back into it."

"It's sporadic for me too, but I run every Saturday and Sunday at eight in the morning," Trish said. She was athletic and pretty from what I could tell behind an apron. "I just run for thirty or forty minutes depending on how I feel. Or how much wine I drank the night before."

I giggled, "I'll take you up on that. You are the first person I've met here. Uh, well, actually the second maybe."

She made a quizzical face as she walked a beer to the other patron. I didn't know if she sensed I was fishing for an invite or if she was just that nice, but my heart jumped at the thought of a running buddy. Rita despised running and all forms of exercise.

"Do you know how to get to the subway, uh, I mean tube from here?" I hollered down the bar to her. Paul was right about making the journey to my office. My first day was in exactly one week and I wanted to get that part over with.

"There's a bus on weekdays," Trish said walking back. "If I see anyone here that takes it, I'll introduce you."

Maybe it was the Guinness or her compassion, but my shoulders visibly dropped from my ears and I felt calm. It's possible that hauling myself and my child across the ocean wasn't a horrible mistake.

A short time later, Trish set a plate of food in front of me full of fish and chips, crab cakes, and fried pickles. She gave me a wink and walked to the other side of the bar. She was already on my top ten list of favorite people in this country. I may only know ten and that includes our driver — but the point being — Trish is awesome.

My hunger took over, and I ate ferociously. Everything tasted so good and I needed some carbs to soak up the beer. Trish walked over with another round while I was eating and leaned her elbows on the counter.

"Milo," she raised her voice towards the door. "Come meet Mel. She needs help with the bus on Monday and maybe forever. Chat with her."

I covered my mouth and turned, chewing quickly to clear my throat to meet my next neighbor.

Shit. Shit. Shit.

We had already met.

Milo, my duplex neighbor, sat at the barstool next to me and swiveled in my direction. His large body shadowed the person on the other side of him, and his forearm took over the entire length of the bar in front of us. He leaned slightly forward with his other hand on his knee and said nothing.

CHAPTER 7

Dear Paul,

May 8th, 2005

I can't begin to tell you how sorry I am to hear about your mother. I don't know what I would do – I've never lost anyone before. That's the wrong thing to tell you – shit. I guess what I'm trying to say is I have no idea how you feel, but I'm here for you.

Except I'm not physically there because I couldn't figure out how to get to London for the funeral. But you know, that being the first time we meet might be weird. I've always wanted to go to London and I'll figure out another way.

This summer isn't going to go as planned, but that's okay. I was excited to meet you and have you summer in Maine, which is the only time you can visit and not get lost under a snowbank. There will be other times though. School has tons of breaks and there is next year.

What a way to graduate - right? Life sure is thrusting you into adulthood. Working with your family sounds good and you all need each other right now.

Thanks for saying my picture was beautiful. You definitely have that royally handsome thing going for yourself. Isn't everyone over there connected to the crown in some way? Just hang on to it - because very soon - when we meet - you will need to know what crazy girl has been annoying you for the past decade.

Countdown to college is on now — or whatever you call it. Why don't you start on some college parties and try to relieve some stress? Meet a hot girl and have her help! You don't need to take over the family responsibilities because you lost a parent. Don't put all that pressure on yourself.

Sorry about your mom (mum) again. I sent you a leather notepad instead of flowers. Flowers die and I find them depressing. It's NOT a diary so don't get all manly about it — but sometimes - writing down what's in your head helps. Like letter writing — how about we do that for the rest of our lives!

Novel idea Mel!

Love,

~~Mel~~

P.S. So — maybe I take back the hot girl comment. Why does that make me a little jealous?

P.P.S. Ignore the jealous comment — just find someone worthy of you is my point.

CHAPTER 8

I grabbed the fresh beer and took a long sip, swallowing hard. There were a few ways I could handle this situation. I could be a total and complete bitch, but Trish was watching. She seemed comfortable with Milo and knew him well enough to volunteer him as tribute for the bus. She smiled at him for Christ's sake, so me being a psycho is a bad plan.

Oblivious dingbat is another option. So lovely to meet you, I'm Mel. Act as if nothing ever transpired and I didn't slam our front door like a sullen teenager.

Or, I could just be myself. I was about two beers in, so transparency was the easiest and most straightforward option. It may also be all I can pull off at this point of inebriation and lack of sleep.

I swung my stool towards him. My knees positioned between his legs. I could cross my legs and accidentally kick him in the balls. Nope, that's Plan A, Mel - bad plan.

I took a visible deep breath in and exhaled slowly. His eyes fluttered down to my chest but quickly recovered.

"What does Milo like to drink?" I gestured my hand to Trish still looking him in the eye. "I'd like to buy him a beer for helping me out."

Trish lifted from the bar and sauntered to the drafts. She didn't sense the tension or maybe she was used to his brooding.

"Maybe we got off on the wrong foot," I said finally shifting my gaze downward. I moved my hands to my lap and started to fiddle. My heart raced as I spoke. I didn't like that he made me nervous and I didn't understand why. He was the jerk and I was being the better person. I gave him enough pause when I realized he wasn't going to respond. "Okay, we did get off on the wrong foot. You were the first person I met moving here, and you were rude to me. I was rude back and that wasn't right. Would you please help me get to the bus Monday?"

Stop talking now Mel or you will ramble forever.

I looked back up at him and resolved to stop fidgeting. He had blue eyes. A stark contrast to his dark hair that he brushed back with his hand before placing it back on his knee. He was wearing the same white shirt and jeans. His expression was unreadable this time. He seemed almost firm. Like he was holding in real emotion and trying to act calm on the outside while boiling on the inside.

Trish dropped two more Guinness's at the bar. Between him and the beer, I may not be able to walk out of here.

Milo lowered his gaze from mine.

"I would like that," he said turning his body back to the bar brushing my knees in the process.

Goosebumps covered my body. I turned towards the bar as well seeing Trish stand with her arms crossed. She looked at Milo and then me, and then back at Milo and then me again like she was at a tennis match. Then she let out a hmpff and started checking on the other customers.

Okay, others feel this interaction is weird too. It's not just a British thing.

Milo drank his beer and ate his food in silence sitting next to me. I nursed my last pint trying to people watch. I texted Rita asking if she needed anything and she promptly replied Not Today Satan. Apparently, she was hellbent on looking as thin as possible in a skimpy dress. By the time I was ready to leave, I felt like I was floating.

I didn't finish my last beer, but exhaustion had worked its magic. I asked Trish to settle, but she said it was taken care of already.

"What do you mean?" I asked, confused.

"It's on the house, love," she answered. "Will I see you tomorrow morning?"

I was glad that she brought it up again. It meant she was genuine about the invite.

"I'm looking forward to it. Where should I meet you?"

"Let me see your phone and I'll text myself. I'm at 13 Winlin, so we can meet out front," she explained reaching for my cell. She typed in numbers quickly and I heard the whoosh of the message. She then grabbed her phone to confirm the receipt. She picked my phone back up and typed again, and another whoosh went through. Milo's phone vibrated.

Oh, God.

"There, now you have Milo's number too for Monday," she said. "Or for …. whatever." She gave me another wink and sauntered off.

I couldn't even look at him, but I felt the burn of him staring at me. He was almost done with his beer, so I needed to scoot out of this awkward situation before he paid as well and we would suffer an uncomfortable walk home to our duplex.

"Thank you so much, Trish," I hollered over to her, stepping off my chair collecting my things. "For the meal and for the kindness. It means a lot. I'll see you Saturday."

I had turned and started towards the door before she responded.

"See you then," she bellowed back as I pushed open the door.

I walked in silence for a few minutes reviewing the events in my head. I would like that, was his response. Why did that excite me? The epitome of pathetic. I'm turning into Rita getting butterflies over a man who hates me and was being polite in front of a friend.

It was a ten-minute walk back to my duplex. I called Rita, but she didn't answer. I shoved the phone in my back pocket and missed dropping it on the concrete. Dammit!

I turned back and dipped down to grab it, and there he was. About ten steps behind me - Milo. He stopped as I stood back up.

"Hey Milo," I said with the most wit anyone can have after a ten-hour flight and two and a half beers.

He shoved his hands in his pockets and took the steps toward me.

"Hello," he replied in a smooth tone. His face had softened completely. His muscles had not, and I felt my breath catch as he got closer.

"Are you gonna go my way?" Okay, my wit was slowly returning to normal.

"Call me Lenny Kravitz," he smiled.

Jesus an actual smile and a joke. It upped his handsome factor immensely. He had perfect teeth to match that strong jawline. Goosebumps and heat covered my body.

We both walked on the small sidewalk side by side. I was fully prepared to embrace the silence. I tried to picture the perfect walk home. He would end up being kind. He just had a headache earlier that made him irritable. He loved having a neighbor, and one with a kid - jackpot! He would offer to help with the bus, tube, and any handyman needs. He would kiss me at the door.

Wait - what?

I reached my hand behind my neck and rubbed it hard trying to hide the tenseness I felt. *Was my chest getting red and blotchy?*

A few silent minutes later we were walking through the blue door, myself first.

"I'll see you later," I muttered rattling my key in the door and stepping in.

The door froze as I tried to push it shut, and I turned to see Milo holding it open with one hand. His head hung down as he rubbed his temples.

Maybe he did have a headache. My door slamming didn't help.

"I was trying to be cold with you," he said softly. His accent making me question if I heard him right.

"C- Cold?" I stuttered. I was facing him completely now, but he didn't lift his head. He seemed almost defeated. Like a man who just lost a championship or his dog.

"Yes, cold," he said, offering no other explanation.

I was completely confused. I needed his help Monday, and he was my neighbor. We needed to be friendly, and his confession made my heart hurt a bit. He was purposely mean.

Should I ask him why? Would it make a difference?

After standing there for what felt like a silent forever, I asked, "And what are you trying to be now?"

He stepped forward moving his hand to my face. I froze in place.

"Closer," he said as he brushed my cheek with his thumb.

CHAPTER 9

Dear Paul,

I hope Nina is feeling better. She's a tough little thing so I'm sure she handled being sick like a champ. When can we have dinner? My treat and bring the whole family. How many years has it been? Let's plan.

I took your advice and went to the bar alone. I met a friend there - Trish. She works at the place and we went running Saturday and Sunday.

Well, she ran and I jogged hyperventilating behind her while she kept having to circle back to get me. She's fast but so sweet. She thinks she can get me to a nine-minute mile in a month, and I'll let her play personal trainer.

We enjoy each other's company and Rita is happy to have the kids while we exercise if I promise never to ask her to go. Also, I'm not allowed to acknowledge if she's wearing the same outfit as the night before when I drop Eva off. So many rules to remember!

Sooooooo I went to the bar alone, but I didn't exactly leave alone. Full circle cliff notes – I met this guy named Milo the first day here and he lives on the other side of the duplex or semi-detached home or whatever you call them. We had a literal run-in where he was kind of a jerk. I then saw him at the Wag, and he got roped into helping me with the tube system Monday. Again, points to me for taking your advice twice now.

Then we walked home together, and he told me he basically was a jerk to me on purpose but now wants to be close to me. The exact word was close. I'm not exaggerating.

What the fuck does that mean?

My reaction – naturally - was to yell out that I had to get my kid. I flew by him, leaving my door open, and walked across the street to get Eva. I then used her as a human shield while I walked home to avoid any interaction with a man.

WHAT'S WRONG WITH ME! Also, what's wrong with him? Why would he be mean on purpose and then decide he wants to be extra nice two hours later.

Sunday, he texted me what time to be ready for the bus the next day, and I was prepared to have an actual conversation. I'm a little embarrassed to say I was excited to see him again. I put on a cute outfit and kept trying to bait him with conversation starters.

He just basically grunted the whole time and avoided eye contact. He wasn't mean, but we didn't get any closer. We never spoke about what happened days before, and it gets stranger.

I managed to locate and take the correct line, and when I made it above ground, he was there. I thought that maybe he worked close to me so whatever.

But THEN when I stopped at the front of my office thrilled that I had made it on my own with little interruption, I saw him again. He was just standing there staring at me.

I walked towards him saying, *Milo - Milo*, but he just walked away.

Now it's Tuesday and I'm thinking of texting him. Is that stupid? He sounds like a crazy stalker, right? Although he doesn't have to work awfully hard because we share a damn wall. Wait, shit, am I the stalker? Maybe this was all coincidence and I'm always right there creepily staring at him.

Anyway, could you please check your calendar and decide on dinner? Rita promises to be on her best behavior.

~~Mel

P.S. I think I like this guy. I feel drawn to him. This is the first time since Mitch. Dinner – SOON – so we can talk about it.

P.P.S. We can talk about you too. It's not all about me I get it.

CHAPTER 10

"Please explain to me why you haven't texted him or just knocked on his damn door yet," Rita snapped holding dresses up to herself. The woman had either already gone shopping or somehow vacuum-packed her entire closet. Outfits were all over her bed and hanging from her standing mirror.

She was going on another date with the guy she met on the plane - Robert. Lynn had given her stamp of approval that he was not a creep and instructed her what restaurants to try - just to be extra careful. Robert had accepted her suggestions with enthusiasm even though they all sounded high dollar.

I had confessed everything to her last night over the phone. She wanted to keep talking about it, but I promised we could spend time together while she got ready and gossip like college girls. I then paced around my house as quietly as possible, so my neighbor didn't know or think I was pacing.

I kept going over our interactions again and again in my mind. Thinking about him made me blush. I had already mapped out the layout of the home in my head using the location of heat, water, and my common sense. I concluded our bedroom and main living area shared the wall. I realized that meant I would hear any female visitors. *What do you care Mel?*

"He's gone from Duplex Dipshit to Duplex Dreamboat in under a week," I replied. "I'm just trying to figure this all out. The red one, you look so good in that one."

"And the girls do too," Rita said shaking her chest at me. "What do you plan on doing with Jack and Eva tonight?"

"I have a puzzle set of London's sights and I got stuff for homemade pizza," I answered.

Rita put her blonde hair back in a clip and started laying out her makeup. "Sounds riveting. So, you will have your phone near you."

"Want me to wing your eyeliner?" I said inspired by her selection of beauty supplies.

"Don't change the subject. And yes. Yes, I do."

We sat cross-legged in front of each other on her floor like we were teenagers and not in our thirties. Rita was naturally beautiful, and she was one of those women that could pull off any outfit or makeup trend.

Before I knew her at work, my eye would be drawn to her in trainings and meetings. She would have fun shoes or red lipstick. Catty girls would make comments about her trying too hard, but I envied her boldness.

Maybe I'm bold now too. Leaving home and starting another chapter.

I grabbed a few of her eyeliners running them through my fingers.

"I get that I'm a broken record, but let me state my case here," she said as she tucked a strand of my hair behind my ear and grabbed my chin. "This is a chance to be a little less sad. But that means you must be a little more daring to get what you want. I don't just mean with your hottie neighbor. This project is huge, and they wanted you. Don't sink back into your old habits in a new country."

I pulled my face away slightly. "I'm definitely daring. I'm here," I said feeling my defenses start to rise. I opened a black eyeliner and placed my pinkie on her forehead to steady my hand. "But I do hear you. I want to change the path I'm on. I want to be recognized for the Prometheus project, and I think I would like to try and maybe, uh, meet someone."

"Haven't you already?" Rita asked.

"I mean maybe someone less, well - intense?" I said shifting back to check my work. The perfect wing.

Rita shot back and clapped her hands. "You mean you want to go out to a bar - a club - the world," she said making small claps.

"Um, well. Maybe yes, I think I would. But not tonight okay. I'm excited about my night in with the kiddos," I chuckled seeing her obvious enthusiasm. This was the moment she was waiting for our entire friendship.

I finished Rita's makeup in a way that only great girlfriends can do. It was what she wanted more than what I would have suggested for her. She looked amazing and almost nervous. This Robert guy must not be a total loser if she cared so much. Good for her, we didn't have to land the plane for her to land a man.

After a few more outfit changes and a predate drink for Rita, I gathered the kids for an errand. Jack, Eva, and I walked down the street holding hands. I carried a large basket of tea, soaps, and potpourri in my arm as we walked.

Mrs. MacArthur had agreed to stay with the children after school and for any nights we wanted to get away. I was anxious to see her before we settled on everything. School started in a few weeks.

Rita had taken Jack down to say hello Saturday morning while I was jogging and raved about her. I hoped my visit was just the silver lining and she had actually looked around the house for things like guns and exposed wires.

I felt my phone buzz in my pocket, but my hands were full. Eva and Jack were talking about what kind of pizza they were going to make. Eva wanted a vegetable on it because I'm raising a middle-aged woman in a seven-year-old body. Jack wanted to know how much cheese counts as extra cheese and how much counts as extra-extra cheese. He was shooting for the bonus extra.

My phone kept buzzing with messages as we walked. Rita was on a roll.

"We're here," I said setting the heavy basket at the front door. "Give me a second kids." I pulled my phone out before knocking.

Tomorrow night we are going out

And I don't want to hear it's a weeknight – I already told Lynn

Oh and ask Mrs. McA if she can watch the kids

What the hell Rita?

Jack stood with his finger lightly touching the buzzer waiting for my signal.

"Okay Jack, GO!" I said. He started buzzing repeatedly and I grabbed his arm away mouthing, that's enough, as Mrs. MacArthur opened the door.

She was shorter than me, but most people are as I stood five foot eight. She was dressed casually in dark cotton pants and a pink sweater. Her white hair was in a loose bun and a diamond pendant hung from her neck. She stepped back from the door and said, "Well, lovely to see you again Jack. Bells are fun, aren't they? When I was a girl, we would ring them and run, but I was naughty."

Jack walked in like he owned the place. Eva paced slowly behind him and waved. "Hello Mrs. MacArthur," she said pining for a hug, which she then got. I already love this woman. *How do the British have the best grandma types?*

Mrs. MacArthur then reached her arms out to me. "You must be the lovely Carmela?" she said. I gave her a hug which I meant to be quick, but I sank into unintentionally. She smelled like tea rose and baked bread. When I entered her home, I immediately knew this was the right place for the kids.

Everything about it was comfortable. Throw blankets and pillows on every chair and sofa. Light green walls were filled with old and new pictures, newspaper articles in frames, and homemade artwork.

There were board games and a stack of children's books on the coffee table. She must have been preparing which was so sweet it made my heart pang. An old record player with a cabinet of records was the only item that made me nervous. I made a mental note to warn the kids about being careful around it later.

The kids had already settled in the living room and grabbed Don't Break the Ice and started stacking the cubes. "Well that's a good sign," I said not realizing I was speaking out loud.

Mrs. MacArthur smiled and started towards her kitchen. "I'll make us some tea. They already know where everything is."

The next hour was an easy conversation like we were already family. She loved Rita and called her a firecracker. She had also known Trish since she was little and let me know she was the kindest soul in town. She wasn't surprised we had become fast friends.

We talked about payment and I realized quickly it would be a fight. She finally agreed to allow me to pay her grocery bill. The kids could eat her out of house and home in snacks. I would leave my card information at the grocer and tell the owner, Bill, that her orders were to be charged to it going forward. Rita and I could settle up later.

I kept wanting to bring up Milo but was too nervous. She could read people and my small-town hunch was correct since she knew the grocer by name. I couldn't tell you the name of one employee at one of our many grocery stores back in Maine.

What if she sensed how I was feeling and said something to Milo?

Instead, I brought up the night out Rita and I were planning, and she offered to watch the kids before I could ask.

I told her I had to get going, but I wanted to stay. She was the kind of woman you talk to about anything. The kids needed to have dinner soon and I was looking forward to the puzzle night. Jack and Eva had moved to *Operation* when I let them know it was time to start picking up.

"I love this wall, Mrs. MacArthur," I said admiring the dozens of frames. "You have a whole life on this wall. Is this just your family?"

"It's so much more than that dear," she said beaming. "This is the article when they finished construction of this estate. Every family wanted to move here, and I was a little girl, so excited. These are my parents. My first cross-stitch is here."

The pictures seemed to move like a timeline. Older black and whites on the left with more recent shots on the right. "Who is down here, your kids or nieces and nephews?"

"Those are my children and underneath are my grandchildren. They all live a few hours away, but I see them often. This is my family here in Winlin. That's Patricia, Trish you know. She was sixteen there, but you see it don't you."

"Are you related?" I asked.

"Oh, no dear," she explained. "But we are all family. So many of us here have been connected by time and we love each other. Like the Masterson family."

I stood up straight. "You know Paul Masterson's family?" I asked. Paul had found Mrs. MacArthur for us, but I thought he just asked around. I didn't know they were family friends. Wouldn't he mention that to me? I was all about myself lately in our letters. "Do they still live here? His family I mean."

Mrs. MacArthur gave me a perplexed smile. "Yes and no," she answered looking over the wall. "There's an estrangement there. I'm sure you understand it's a private matter."

"Oh yes, I do. I'm sorry I didn't mean to intrude." I felt uneasy. How much did I truly know Paul? "Okay, kids you ready to go?" They had whined a bit about leaving, much to the adults' pleasure. The kids gave her hugs and started through the door.

"Oh well here's someone you are acquainted with." Mrs. MacArthur had lifted a picture from the wall holding it out to me and gave me a sweet smile.

It was a young man sitting outside on a porch chair. It looked like one of the Winlin houses with a brightly colored door in the background. He was relaxed and smiling with a drink in one hand. He was maybe in his twenties when the picture was taken. Dark hair, strong jaw, and broad chest. My heart fluttered and my cheeks flushed.

It was Milo.

Younger, less angry, but definitely Milo.

"That's what I thought," she whispered.

CHAPTER 11

Dear Paul,

June 5th, 2009

Well, I'm back together with Mitch again. I don't know what I'm doing. It's just easy, I guess. No drama. As you know I've had my fill of men that are drama. After getting hit by a man, sometimes boring is nice. I need simple. I need comfortable. I need reliable.

He knows the food I like to eat – what movie I'll want to see at the theater. Now sex has gotten kind of – you know – the same. It's more like a race to orgasm so he can watch something on TV, but everyone says that's how long-term relationships are.

He thinks you hate him. I told him you met some hottie at school and you are basically living together. Which, for the record, I told you would happen. First, she leaves a hairbrush and then some deodorant. Then she has a drawer, and POOF, you are in a relationship pal.

How's monogamy feel? Does it feel like you are about to buy a house and get a dog? Does it feel like a diamond, my friend?

Summer has started by the way. Not sure if you could tell through the English fog. This is the last chance before we have to start our actual lives. Are we meeting? This just seems like the beginning of the end. I hate how you wrote in your last letter that you feel like I'm slipping away. At first, I was pissed and then I realized I hadn't written in three weeks because I was busy. I don't want to fade away from you.

How busy are we going to be with yards to mow and real jobs and – Jesus what if we have kids? I don't want to lose what we have. You are my longest relationship. You are the first person to love me outside of my family.

I appreciate the offer to send money to get me over there, but I have some saved. Just get me a place to stay and I'll look at the dates you gave me. This is going to happen. Mitch can get the fuck over it.

I'm fine to stay with you, but your girlfriend may be pissed about it. How would she feel about me coming at all? This may be harsh – don't show her this letter – but I don't care.

So, anyway – this letter was primarily to confess I've fallen back into the Mitch situation. I appreciate in advance you not giving me shit about it.

I'll write to you soon when I get my travel plans figured out. I can't wait to see you!

Love,

Mel

CHAPTER 12

My heels clicked on the street as we hurried in the brisk air. We were about thirty minutes from home, but I wasn't entirely sure where. I could hear music from the outside, and for the first time, it made me want to dance not run. This would be fun.

"There he is," Rita squealed waving down the street. "Stay right here this is the place." She walked quickly with little steps in her tight blue dress, I assumed towards Robert. He gave a little jog towards her and they kissed meeting halfway. He was handsome - a banker or lawyer-type. He held her hand walking and couldn't take his eyes off her.

I caught my reflection in the window of the club. My dress was black, mid-thigh, and fitted. It hugged my curves and cinched in at the waist. A deep V in the front showed maybe a little too much cleavage, but I had the right bra for it. I had managed to get my thick dark hair in an array of full long curls. Overall, I felt good and it was showing.

"This is Robert," Rita beamed. He stretched out a hand.

"It's so nice to meet you," I said as we shook. He looked over at Rita. He wanted to please her by making a good impression. She nodded in approval at him.

"I reserved a table here," Robert said leading us inside. He had his hand on the small of Rita's back as I trailed behind them. "It's a great spot. We can all dance and have a place to go back and relax, eat, and drink."

The club was stunning. I was shocked at how much bigger it was than I thought from outside. We entered in on the second floor. Ropes lined the walls leading to a large staircase that made its way down to the dance floor on the lower level. Bars were lined on the outside walls of the bottom floor and it was horribly crowded down there. The DJ lifted above the crowd in the center on a circular platform.

As we made our way to the staircase, a rope lifted on the left, and a large man dressed in a black suit ushered Robert inside. I followed, thankful that I didn't have to be shoved into the mass of people yet. Just inside a young girl held up a platter of champagne flutes and I didn't hesitate to grab a glass. I would need some liquid courage to get downstairs later.

The second floor was decadent and overdone in a way only a nightclub can get away with. There were heavy curtains lining rooms that peppered the entire floor. Some were pulled back showing groups of people deep in chatter and laughter. Heavy oak furniture with plush sofas filled the rooms. Large art pieces hung on the walls, and the ceiling was painted like Starry Night.

When we entered our reserved area a bottle of champagne was already on the table with chocolate-covered strawberries. A bit over the top but Rita was swooning. Robert took gold bracelets from a dish on the table and handed them to us. "These will allow you to come and go," he explained.

A waitress in a small skirt shot over with purpose. She was on a mission as she started emptying her tray of champagne glasses. She set the tray to the side and grabbed a knife from her belt and said, "Ready for the champagne?"

We all nodded in agreement a little hesitant of the giant knife such a small woman was holding. She grabbed the bottle with her left hand around the base and pointed herself away from us. One slice of the knife across the length of the bottle was all it took.

Champagne sprayed from the top while Rita and I clapped in amazement. She filled our drinks - spoke to Robert for a moment - and skirted away. I held Rita's hand and squeezed it. Already the night was turning out to be the most fun I've had in a long time.

The drinks came frequently and went down easily. Robert had a few friends stop by and chat with us. Everyone was funny and talkative. Lynn came by with her husband and I was relieved to now know two people at the office before my first day.

"Let's go dance," Lynn said standing up and pulling Rita's hand with her. "You too Mel."

"I think I've had enough to agree to that," I giggled scooting off the sofa.

I thought we were headed back to the stairs, but Lynn led us to an elevator a few tables down. When we exited another rope led us onto the dance floor. There must have been the best sound engineers designing the place because the music was booming on the first floor, while it was barely thudding on the second.

The base felt good and we started dancing as we walked out. Waitresses whisked through the crowds with ease and another drink entered my hand.

"I didn't order this," I yelled to her over the music. She responded by running her finger along my gold bracelet. Lynn gave me a wink while she shook her wrist. I could get used to this. Play on Rita.

I had no idea how long we were dancing, but each song sounded better than the last one. A mist of sweat was on my chest and forehead. Lynn's husband and Robert had ventured down, and I was dancing with them but not with them at the same time.

I didn't realize it when I was drifting further into the crowd. A man who was attractive and not too grabby started dancing with me, so I went along. Then another man came up behind me and the same deal. Moments later, I looked around but didn't see Rita and Lynn. The floor had a huge blind spot with the DJ platform in the center. I was sure they were on the other side or maybe they went back upstairs.

All the drinks that helped me feel carefree just a moment ago, now made me fuzzy. An arm was around my waist, and I didn't recognize the man attached to it. It was time to exit.

"I need to get to the elevator," I shouted to him.

"There's no elevator here," he bellowed back.

"There is, but I can find it myself. I have to go. Thanks for the dance." His arm tightened around me as I started away and I was pulled back. "Your cute, but seriously, I need to find my friends."

"I could be your friend," he said pulling tighter.

"No thanks," I put my hands on his chest and tried to straighten my arms to push myself away. He pulled tighter and reached his hand down my backside cupping my ass.

My blood started pumping in my ears and my body began to tingle with adrenaline. There's a moment when a woman knows she's outpowered. She can scream. She can fight. But she can feel it. The strength of a man holding her that she can't overcome. The sensation washed over me.

An arm shot between us and a hand wrapped around the guy's neck. His grip on me immediately loosened and I stumbled backward. Their faces were inches apart.

Milo?

They struggled slightly, but Milo had a grip on the guy's throat so tight all he could do was thrash at his arm begging for release. Accepting defeat, the lesser man brought his hands up in surrender and was pushed away by his neck.

"Are you okay?" he barked coming towards me. Security was behind him and the sight of so many large fuming men was frightening.

I kept walking backward not looking where I was going. I mis stepped on the edge of the dance floor and teetered back. Milo grabbed my hand and pulled me towards him and into his arms.

His grip around me was tight and I melted. I could feel his heart pounding in his chest. He was upset, almost shaking as he held me.

"Are you okay," he asked again in my ear.

"Milo," I sighed. "What are you doing here?"

CHAPTER 13

Milo shifted his arm around my waist and began walking. I didn't know where we were going. I was staring at him and didn't care. His jaw was so tight I thought his teeth would crack. The veins in his neck were pulsing and he was radiating heat.

He was disheveled, not dressed for a club like this. I was surprised they even let him in. He had on a dark khaki cargo jacket with a black shirt and jeans. His dark hair wasn't slicked back and kept falling over his forehead.

We were walking through the kitchen, his grip on me tighter now as we weaved through the stainless-steel counters and cooking staff. They didn't seem to notice us or care, but I distinctly thought I heard a man say, *hey boss*.

When we made it to the back, someone opened the door for Milo, and we were suddenly thrust outside into the chilly night. We weren't in a side ally, but more of an outdoor break area. There were a few tables and chairs lined against the brick. I guessed this was for staff only.

I crossed my arms around my chest suddenly cold from the sweat and my tiny dress. Milo took off his jacket and draped it around me. He then started to pace.

"Rita and Lynn, they-they d-don't know where I am," I stuttered. "I didn't bring my phone. They could be looking for me."

He stopped pacing and rushed towards me. I instinctively backed up against the brick wall. "They weren't concerned when that asshole was grabbing at you." Milo spit out. He was so close I could feel the warmth radiating off his body. "They seemed just fine by themselves not giving a shit about what happened to you."

His words were shocking. The rage behind them and the truth of them. I felt ashamed. I was alone here. Alone again thinking I had this great new support system. It was like I was back at my uncle's house. Same story, different country.

Before I could help it the tears silently rolled down. I didn't sniffle or cry audibly, but I could feel them drop down my cheeks. I had made poor decisions tonight - drinking too much and putting my faith in people I didn't know.

"You're right," I said. "I need to look out for myself, and I didn't."

The tension left his body. His face fell and he lifted his hand to my cheeks and rubbed his thumbs over my tears. "I didn't mean to make you cry," he whispered. "I would never want to do that. You scared me tonight."

I grabbed his wrist to stop his touch. "What are you doing here Milo? After avoiding me, ignoring me."

He said nothing. Just stepped closer. I could hear our breathing. Loud hard breaths as we stood against one another. My chest now rising and falling against him.

He moved his hand underneath his jacket, around my waist, pressing our bodies together.

"I've had some conflicts with myself when it comes to you. I should let you be, but I've realized that's not possible," he admitted.

His lips met mine. Soft at first, barely a touch. Then harder pulling me closer. I had released his wrist and both of his hands now moved over my body. I could feel his muscles flexing through my thin dress. I didn't question or fight it. I couldn't even if I wanted to, and I didn't want to.

His tongue entered my mouth and I opened moaning softly. Our kissing now in rhythm, but still frantic. My hands raced up his chest and slid behind his neck. I had my fingers in his hair as he moved down my neck kissing and nibbling my exposed skin.

I could feel him hard through his jeans pressing into my stomach. Holy shit this man was hung. It seemed like my legs would give out from underneath me. I was trembling as his hand moved down my thigh and then slid under my dress. His lips moved back to my mouth slowly pressing his tongue back inside.

His hand moved over my bare ass and then to my hips. His fingers hooked the top of my panties. I felt him pull slightly down and then he paused. We continued to kiss as I waited. The anticipation was exciting and terrifying.

What is he doing?

What am I doing?

He slowly stretched his hand open and slid his palm back down my leg and out of my dress.

Without realizing it or meaning to, I whimpered. I wanted him and it was obvious to both of us now. The desperation in our kiss was still there, but I started to release myself. I needed him to stop, or him inside me. One of those wasn't possible tonight.

He cupped my face and tilted my head back. We stayed there for a moment breathing heavily until he finally spoke.

"You asked why I'm here Mel. Now you know."

CHAPTER 14

Dear Mel,

I have to make a confession and you aren't going to like it. Before I absolve myself, please know everyone is doing great and Nina is already much better. I appreciate your offer to take us all out to dinner.

My confession is I don't know how dinner could happen at this point. I don't know how to start really. I don't know how to explain it.

Letters as of late have been focused on you, and I mean that in the kindest way possible. You have had a wild couple of months, and it's allowed me some time to try and sort this mess out. To sort our situation out.

I haven't had to address this issue. I should scrap this paper and start over, but maybe not. My rambling could prove my confusion.

Claudia would not agree to dinner. I'm trying to work it out. The reason our mail goes to a post office box isn't that we had identity theft all those years ago. She doesn't approve of our correspondence.

It's such a long story. I don't want to get into it just yet. I'm hoping we can have an in-person meeting in the future and I can explain. In short, she told me to stop writing to you when she and I were having marital troubles. At that time, the letters were few and far between.

I came to a solution so we could keep in touch with each other. I'll leave it at that for now.

I did confess the situation when you decided to come to London. I don't believe you will be here for only six months, so I told her the letters continued. Your company has a history of relocating employees permanently after a temporary stay. I also happen to think it is the best thing for you and Eva.

Every letter since Mitch died was laced with a sad memory or regret. I don't think you even knew it or saw it. It burned me how you blamed yourself. How others felt the need to tell you what they would have done. How they would have made an impossible choice. Here you can love the good memories from afar.

America was your purgatory. Don't go back.

Just know I'm working this out. I'll find a way, but I need to sort out some things with Claudia. It's not a lost cause, but I know you may have expected me at the airport or something gallant like that. I've disappointed you, and I'm sorry.

Our friendship means so much to me. I'll get myself figured out.

I may throw this letter into the rubbish. If it's very crumpled, I dug it out again.

~~Paul

P.S. Mrs. MacArthur rang, and she adores the children.

P.P.S. Men aren't great at faking anything (unlike women, as you explained). When we can't understand or express our feelings, we close ourselves off.

CHAPTER 15

It was like being a teenager on the first day of school. Rita and I waited on the corner ready for the bus. I had on a brand-new black pencil skirt and a silky white crossbody blouse. The laptop bag I ordered had come in, although it was sans laptop. Instead of coffee, I brought a water bottle, considering the white top may not survive the bus and subway and walking in general with coffee. *Not to mention you've already had three cups, Mel.*

I stumbled onto the bus proving my point already. Rita patted my booty from behind being playful as we made our way in. Last night we had our first argument in England which was rather good honestly - considering the stressful move. It didn't last long with Rita apologizing and bursting into tears about five minutes in.

Milo had walked me back into the club after our outdoor encounter. His answer to my question left me with a hundred more, but I was too flustered to ask them. When I collected my things from the table and called Rita, she didn't answer. Twenty minutes of searching for her and nothing.

After I felt like I had given an honest effort, Milo put me in a car home. I was disappointed he wasn't coming with me but didn't ask why not. The kids were spending the night at Mrs. MacArthur's so I fell asleep in my dress thinking about Milo's hands and mouth.

The next morning, I went to Rita's house with coffee. Robert answered the door heading out himself. After some smart-ass remarks on my part with passive-aggressive comments on hers - an actual fight started between us. It ended when I tearfully told her I felt unsafe the night before and I needed her. She cried and apologized promising to duct tape her phone to her next time and have one of us sober whenever we went anywhere again.

When I got home and checked my mail, I found Paul's letter in my mailbox – postmarked this time. With so much to process, I took the day to cuddle up with a book (and wine) while Eva did crafts and watched her tablet.

I did take the end of Paul's letter to heart and texted Milo. I didn't want him to close off again. I decided to start with something safe. I've been thinking about you nonstop and don't want you to disappear again, seemed a bit desperate.

> *Did you get home alright last night?*

> *Yes, when can I see you again?*

Okay, so he was going right in.

> *I'm home*

And now I'm going right in.

> *I'm not home. I won't be until late – hours away. Tomorrow?*

My first day of work is tomorrow. After?

I'll see you on the bus. Then lunch. Text me what time I'll come to your building.

I decided to be a little coy and see how forthcoming he would be.

Do you know where my building is?

You know I do

A shiver went down my spine. I put my phone away deciding I would leave the conversation on a high note.

I woke up in the middle of the night to his footsteps. When I looked at my phone it was 2 AM. It took me forever to fall asleep in the first place - so I forced myself back to bed. I did make sure I didn't hear anyone else with him though. *Because you care Mel.*

I shifted in my seat as our commute continued. "Hey so I can't do lunch today," I said to Rita as she slid closer to me and further from the stranger to her right.

"Okay," she said pausing before she continued. "You know we are all working smarter not harder. You don't need to work through lunch on the first day to set a precedent."

I bit my lip. "That's not it at all. I'm going to lunch with Milo."

"What!" Rita turned with a catlike grin.

"I have to catch you up on a lot. It's been a wild forty-eight hours and I didn't fill you in on everything yet."

"We have a long commute," Rita said now sitting at attention. "Spill it. I have some things to catch you up on too."

"Oh, I think I know. I saw Robert coming out yesterday, remember?"

She giggled, "It's more than that. But you first."

I realized Milo would be getting on at the next stop. When we rode together the first time, we met at Winlin Wag. Trish had mentioned the bar opened for breakfast and he was there most days. There was no way I could talk about him only a row or two in front of us.

"Paul wrote me this disturbing letter," I muttered. "I brought it. Here."

Rita took the letter as the bus began to slow and then stopped. I could see Milo out the window talking with another man. He was dressed business casual in black pants, a collared shirt, and no tie. I could see the broadness of his back and his hair was combed out of his eyes. Clean-shaven and holding a cup of coffee - he boarded looking edible.

I regretted not calling Rita last night and telling her everything. Maybe then she would move her seat so I could have him near me - have him touch me again.

Milo sought me out as he boarded and caught my eye. I smiled and he grinned in return. He noticed Rita reading the letter, her mouth agape at what she was seeing.

His expression immediately hardened. I looked back and forth between them, but he didn't seem to notice. He was steely-eyed towards the piece of paper in Rita's hand. The man next to him started tapping on his shoulder asking him something. He eventually turned back and answered him, engaging in a conversation.

Sorry we can't sit together. I texted him.

He didn't seem to notice his phone buzz or look down at anything. Maybe it was off.

"This is insane," Rita said when she finished reading. "I knew his wife was batshit crazy. You've been sending letters to a post office box this whole time. What the hell? You could have been catfished."

"Shhhhhh," I said pleading with her to be quiet. I had no idea how well Milo could hear two rows away. "I don't know what to make of it. I knew his wife didn't want us to talk on the phone or video chat, but I had no idea it went this deep."

"It's because he wants to go deep," Rita chuckled at her joke. The man next to her looked up from his phone.

"We've never been – you know – romantic or anything. We love each other but it's not like that." I didn't confess that I was never really sure about the romance part with Paul. We used to sign our letters with love and often admitted jealousy when talking about dating other people. It was always an unanswered question – how far it could go if we had let it – if we had ever met.

"Because you have never talked period. Get you two in a room and I guarantee it goes beyond friends. Claudia was right to cut that off first. I'll give her that."

"So, the friend I've had for over twenty years is only an hour or so away and I don't meet him. That makes zero sense. What do I write back to this?"

Rita folded the letter back and put it in the envelope. She sat back with a huff. "I'll have to think about that. But in the meantime, I'm emailing him."

"Emailing him what Rita?" I asked sternly. "I don't want him to know you read this."

She waved her hand in my face. "You think I'm an amateur? I'll ask him to go to dinner with me and Robert. Wait, oh my oh my oh my."

"What," I said panicky. "What happened?"

"His IP address Mel. We can trace it now."

"Anyone can trace an IP address. It gives the city and a general area. I know he's in this city hence my frustration."

"So close yet so far, girl, I get it, but Prometheus gives us spy level access," she continued. "I've read the business plan. It's marketing with pinpoint precision. Targeting the people's shopping and social media down to their street, even in their damn house. Aaaaand we have a dedicated IT department with twelve people."

"Just stop," I said. "There's a better way than going full stalker. What would I do? Find him and show up on his doorstep. Claudia would shoot me on the spot."

"I'm just giving ideas here. I'll be sure to make nice with an IT guy before Robert and I get exclusive. "

I turned my head so fast my neck popped. "Exclusive?" Rita hadn't been monogamous since I'd known her. She started to blush and shrugged her shoulders.

"I need to catch you up too, girl," she said smiling broadly. "But honestly, how many times did you read that letter."

I let out a hard breath and frowned. "Maybe a hundred. I'm less upset because I'm excited about, uh, lunch plans you know. But I'm sad about this. I thought we were like, best friends, you know."

"I get it. He said himself in the letter, he'll figure this out. It's not over. Also, I'm your best friend. I called it - like the front seat."

"Subject change," I said lifting my finger. "What's going on with you."

We spent the rest of the commute engrossed in Rita's whirlwind romance. She was enamored with Robert, and from the sounds of it, he felt the same way. He encouraged her to find Jack's dad. Robert never knew his father and understood Jack would want that one day. Rita found that empathetic and endearing. There wasn't much about Robert she didn't like. Aside from Jack, Robert's heart and dick seemed to be her new favorite things on the planet. The poor man next to us got an earful.

I spent a lot of the ride listening and watching. Watching Milo from the back of the bus specifically. He never took out his phone from what I could tell, and he didn't turn to me again. He was doing something with paperwork in his lap and occasionally spoke to the man next to him to be polite.

When we reached our destination, traffic had delayed us for about fifteen minutes. Fifteen minutes meant Rita and I were doing a quick sprint to the tube, so we weren't delayed another twenty waiting for the next one. Being thrust in the crowds of people meant I lost Milo. Rita had grabbed my hand and started to run so I had no choice but to follow instead of looking for him like a lost puppy.

I forgot about my disappointment when we made it to our office floor a few minutes early. It was time to focus on the reason I moved to London.

The entire area was an open floor plan with shades of teal and bright blue. All the offices were fishbowls, but I knew you could move them to opaque with the click of a button. Same design plan as the US office.

Lynn rushed over when we stepped onto the floor. She had been waiting to greet us and to apologize to me for the other night. I waved her off as she hugged me and said it wouldn't ever happen again. Neither of them knew I was whisked away by my handsome neighbor and their guilt wasn't entirely justified. They should feel bad, just not this bad - *maybe*.

"I volunteered to give you the morning tour," Lynn said as she started walking us through the floor. "I'll take you to your office first so you can set your stuff down."

Rita and I shared a Jack and Jill office space. We each had a separate entry to the glass-encased rectangle, with a shared meeting room that could fit eight people comfortably. The room had a projector, laptop, whiteboards, and fridge. Our separate offices were stylish and simple. We each had a large white desk with an extra monitor, bookshelves on the wall, and the most amazing view of London.

The floor had a snack station with fresh fruits and bakery items delivered daily. They were complimentary along with every kind of coffee and tea imaginable if you could figure out the machine.

I could be a barista if it meant free delicious coffee.

We met everyone on the floor and no one had name tags, which was a nightmare for me. Rita would be a social butterfly and catch me up. There were a couple of Americans and Australians who assured us living here was the most amazing decision. *Maybe Paul was right about the relocation tactics.*

Lynn then brought us to the support team, and a young man walked back with us to our offices to set up our new laptops. Before I knew it, I felt my stomach churn. It was 12:30 and all I had today was my coffee and bottled water. Rita gave me a small wave as she scurried past my wall. She had her bag and was on the phone with Robert no doubt.

I texted Milo that I was leaving for lunch and started collecting my things. When I had made it back downstairs and across the lobby, I frowned to see that he hadn't texted back. Not that I was expecting him to be waiting by the phone. But yeah, I was expecting him to be waiting by the phone.

I paced my lobby a bit and decided I couldn't waste my day on a man. The hot and cold bullshit had to stop. You want me or you don't – and I certainly don't have any more time in this life to deal with men who can't figure that out until it's too late. Life is too short, and I knew that all too well.

CHAPTER 16

Dear Mel,

14th December 2009

Happy Christmas Mel. I hope you and Mitch are having a great holiday. Claudia and I will be going to the Isles later in the month instead of having a large family holiday. I love my brothers and my dad, but she has a point. It's always a fight when we are together. They don't particularly care for her as of late. I don't see why. She's never done anything vile towards them.

It will be odd to spend the holiday without them, but it will be a nice change of pace. We can start our own traditions. She expects a ring you know - you were right about that. She leaves post all over the flat open to pages of three-carat princess cuts. I'm a bit clueless, but not daft. I don't think we are ready, but she's the only good thing I have going right now.

Business is horrid. My father had more vested in American properties than we originally thought and we can't pull out of those just yet. He's starting to become forgetful to a point where we need to hire a full-time aide. I'm not pleased with what's been provided so we are tightening the wallets to make it work. We need a proper accountant. Claudia helps where she can, but the lack of cash flow keeps me up at night.

Sorry to complain, but while we are on negative topics – I'll address your last letter. Perhaps the last five where you continue to bring up how you stood me up this year? I haven't written about it because I wasn't ready to, but let's close the year with that chapter and leave it to die.

You broke my heart with your false promises. I needed you this year. What kept me going through everything was knowing I would see you. It's obvious that's never going to happen.

You said fate doesn't have it in the cards. Bollocks to fate. You chose not to come.

Mitch refused to travel, but he would leave you if you did. Does that sound healthy to you? Claudia isn't thrilled with our friendship – and I've paid dearly for that. Many arguments center around my connection to you, but I kept firm that you were part of the package.

A part of me broke this year. You are more important to me than I am to you. I need to evaluate things with myself and figure out why that is. I need to work on my relationship with Claudia.

Give us Christmas to have some time away from reality. Write to me in the new year and we can start fresh. I don't want to write about this again. I want to move forward. 2010 will be a chance for a new beginning.

Spend this time with Mitch and give my love to your family. A little separation may do us both some good.

I love you,

Paul

CHAPTER 17

When I stepped outside Milo was seated on the benches by the front doors. He had a large paper sack next to him and grinned when he saw me. *Well shit drama queen.*

"You could have texted me back at some point today," I said walking up to him with a tight smile.

He hit a button on his phone and my cell vibrated.

> *I'm waiting outside gorgeous. I brought sandwiches and salads. You can take home what you don't want for Eva.*

"Ah well still a little late," I said after reading his message. I hesitated for a moment perplexed. "Did I tell you my daughter's name? I mean, we just haven't discussed my daughter. I didn't know you knew her name."

"Of course, you did," Milo said standing reaching for my hand. "Shall we go?"

I felt silly, but it bothered me that I couldn't place where I had discussed Eva with him by name. He knew her existence, and that couldn't be avoided. I didn't like the thought of my daughter meeting men before I was sure they would be around forever. Forever is a loose term considering my history, but I wanted to limit her heartaches. Milo living next door and the entire Winlin community in everyone's business, I couldn't help that he knew about her already.

"Where are we going," I asked. It was a beautiful day and the leaves had started to turn. No rain was in sight which was a first since I'd been here.

"There's a restaurant a few steps from here. It's only open for dinner so we can sit on their patio. Are you alright to eat outside?" *I was alright to do anything if he kept talking with that accent.*

"And they will let us?" I should be letting him take the lead, but I didn't want to be in some sort of trouble on my first day of work. Sorry, I'm late. Scotland Yard picked me up for trespassing.

Milo's smile widened. "It won't be a problem."

"You have a strange way of answering questions you know," I said squeezing his hand.

"Really? I've answered all your questions so far."

"With one-word answers Milo. Two huge questions you answered with literally a syllable."

"Were the answers unclear? Is there something more you need to ask?"

I thought about that a moment. They weren't unclear. They were probably more direct than any man had ever been, but that didn't mean I understood them. *And absolutely Milo - there are more things I need to ask.*

Milo led me through a black garden gate on the side of a building. Flowers were lining the walkway which led to outdoor tables. We were alone here which made my body hum remembering the last time he had me on my own outside. A man from the restaurant opened the back door to the patio - waved to Milo - then stepped back inside.

Well okay, that's kind of weird.

"They weren't unclear," I said as we started to unpack our lunch. Milo pulled out my chair and then sat down next to me instead of across from me. "They just led to more questions is all."

"So, ask them," he responded with calm assurance in his voice.

"Okay," I started to poke around my salad unsure of where to start. "Why were you cold the first day I moved in?"

Milo put his hand on my thigh where my skirt met my skin. He started rubbing circles with his thumb raising my skirt slightly in the process. "A friend was upset that you were living in the other half of my house. We fought about it just minutes before you arrived."

"A female friend?"

"No."

I exhaled in relief and continued, "I get that would put you in a bad mood, but how would you have any control over that?"

"I own our home. I choose to have a renter or not. He didn't

77

think it would be a good situation."

"I see," I said, deciding to finally start in on my salad. He wasn't telling me everything, but I was satisfied that his rudeness wasn't completely about me, Mel the person, more like me in existence in his personal space.

He ate for a moment with one hand, never lifting his other from my thigh.

"I have a question for you," he said. He was struggling to ask this - I could tell. His jaw had tightened, and his eyes narrowed at his food. "What was your friend, the blonde, reading on our commute this morning?"

What? Of all the things to ask I didn't expect that.

"Rita," I said. "She moved here with me, and she has a son, Jack."

He didn't look up from his meal and didn't reply giving a slight nod. He wasn't interested in learning about Rita, he was waiting for his answer.

"Um, a letter. Something a friend had written to me. Why?"

"I just want to know more about you," he smiled tightly towards me. He was then quiet in a way that makes you want to ramble. I felt the need to explain myself about Paul's letter, but like hell I was going down that road. This may be our first official date and I'm not spending it talking about another man.

"I want to know more about you too," I said uncrossing my legs. His hand shifted upwards and I pretended not to notice. I could feel the heat between my thighs. *Could he?* "Have you always lived on Winlin?" I knew the answer but had to start somewhere.

"I was born in Mrs. MacArthur's house," he said nonchalantly. "My mother knew she wouldn't make it to the hospital, so she went there."

I must have had a confused look on my face, so he continued. "Mrs. MacArthur is a midwife. She delivered half of the community. A good choice for childcare."

"Oh wow, I didn't know. I mean she's our babysitter so that's good to hear," I carried on, embarrassed it never came up in our conversation the other day. "Did I tell you she was our babysitter?"

He wiped his face with a napkin and moved closer to me, his hand moving further, now completely under my skirt. His thumb continued the slow circles. I felt myself tense and my breath catch. My heart was beating out of my chest every time he moved that damn hand.

"I'm very perceptive," he said leaning in towards me nipping my neck. "I notice things. Especially beautiful things that are right outside my door."

I had completely given up on my lunch now. My hands were white-knuckled on the edge of the table as my breathing quickened. He moved further inside of my skirt, shifting his other to graze the outside of my thigh pulling the fabric up. I lifted myself slightly and when I came back down, he had full access to every part of me.

"Are there people inside the restaurant that can see us?" I panted. I still had my grip on the table as he reached to the back of my head, lightly gripped my hair, and bit my neck. I wasn't sure who I was anymore. This woman who bared herself to a man she barely knew did not exist in Maine. I had an expiration date on my life here - and it gave me a sense of anonymity. Who would I see again after this spring came and went? These could be wild stories I told my grandchildren one day.

"Don't look around, look at me," he said pushing my lips to his and kissing me gently. The way he kissed me gave a sense of closeness I couldn't imagine after Mitch. He felt like home, but we were nowhere near any home old or new. This feeling - this moment - this man was completely foreign to me. So why was I so comfortable with him?

He had found his way to my panties now, but this time he didn't hesitate. I felt them rip as he yanked, and his fingers then entered my flesh.

I yelped in surprise, and he broke our kiss resting his forehead on mine. "Did I hurt you?" he breathed almost into my mouth, but not stopping. He kept moving in and out of me while he waited for my reply.

"No, um, no," I gasped unable to make a coherent sentence. *A man literally ripped my panties off me. This could not be reality.*

He didn't wait for more detail and his lips were on mine in almost desperation. His tongue moving through my mouth like he couldn't breathe if he weren't kissing me. The intensity made me forget everything around me. People could have walked up and started clapping and all I would see and feel is Milo.

It wasn't long before I had no control over our embrace. I just moaned in his mouth while he worked me. Sensing my loss of composure, he moved his mouth down my neck continuing his rhythm. My head laid on his shoulder while I wrapped my arms around him. When he brought his thumb to my clit, I bit his shoulder so I wouldn't scream out.

Nothing stopped his pace as I squeezed his body tighter feeling the tension rise in me. I began to dig into his back rocking my body back and forth with his movements. He followed, not letting up. He began to moan deeply with my tiny shakes.

"Come for me," he commanded in my ear. "Now Carmela."

I felt the rise of my orgasm rip through me as I shuddered violently in his arms. My entire body hitting its peak as I screamed into his shoulder desperately trying to muffle my release. The wave was so intense I felt tears well up in my eyes.

When I finished shaking, he removed his hand while I lay limp in his arms. He gently kissed my neck moving to my chin and my mouth trying to coax me back to the land of the living. I blinked quickly trying to recover from almost crying. *Not sexy Mel, pull yourself together.*

He looked into my eyes with calmness now. He had caught his breath and rubbed my back with the palm of his hand. I stared back at him with a mix of confusion and contentment. He was so gorgeous - I could stay like this forever.

But the little voice in the back of my head started its nagging. The noise that tells you something is off. I don't know him well enough. I don't know him at all. Confusion was an understatement. I had to start digging before it was too late to say no to him. Maybe it already was.

CHAPTER 18

When I came back to work, I looked properly tousled. My hair was a bit more than windblown and my skirt was wrinkled. The look on Rita's face was priceless. I quickly locked both doors to my office to buy some time before she barged in.

She gave the handle a few good shakes, but just when I thought she gave up a note slid from underneath the conference room door.

How was your ~~FUCK~~*. I'm sorry I meant how was your lunch.*

I couldn't help but feel the rush from the past hour. All the sensations came back and made my cheeks burn hot. For the rest of our lunch, we sat side by side with our legs touching. I'm not sure how much we both ate, but the conversation was smooth without awkwardness between us.

I didn't pry too much but asked some starter questions so I could investigate later. I started with his last name which he took a moment to answer. I didn't know if it's because he didn't want to or because he just realized he was finger banging someone who didn't know his last name.

Milo Bennett was two years older than me. He had never been married and had no children. I didn't dare ask if he wanted any, and besides, that would tell me about his future and right now I had to focus on his past. He has brothers. Not sure how many yet. His father is in a home and his mother died when he was very young.

Once I had the family history it was time to walk back into my building. He asked a few questions about me, but most of the conversation was my interview. I would give more of myself next time, but for now, I had what I needed to start.

I flipped the paper over, wrote Rita a note as she tapped her shoe on the other side of the door, and slid the paper back.

It's been 5 hours. Did you get a ~~hot~~, I'm sorry I mean smart IT guy to help us yet?

I heard her squeal on the other side of the door and I unlocked it.

"If you think this message is going to stop me from playing ninety-nine questions about your lunch, you have yet again - miscalculated," she said barging in and taking a seat in my desk chair. She leaned back and crossed her legs giving a little spin.

"Not here," I replied sternly. "I WILL catch you up, and it WILL be worth it, but I can't discuss this at work. We have our People Team orientation in twenty minutes anyway."

"Okay good, half the IT team is new and will be there. We can get someone to smoke out Paul," Rita smiled pleased with the idea of my coming around.

"Not Paul. Milo."

Rita stopped her gentle spinning with one heel. "Most people start with a google search of the new boyfriend. Maybe a criminal background check if you are extra."

"Okay not my boyfriend, and there's something there Rita. Something he's not telling me. I get this feeling. Like you know when the woman says there was a hint that her husband was cheating, but she could never put her finger on it, and the bastard has a whole other wife and kids somewhere."

Rita looked at me deadpan. "I don't think this is like that Mel. You okay?"

"That's extreme I know. I'm just saying he's purposely allusive. Lying by omission maybe."

"You could just date him and get to know him. Crazy idea I know, but I'm just throwing spaghetti on the wall here. Let's see if it sticks."

Rita threw a pencil at me with a light toss. I stood with my arms crossed as it hit my chest and fell to the ground. She sulked and sat back in my chair. Grabbing a tissue, she started to wave it like a white flag. "I give. Whatever makes you comfortable. But we are searching Paul too. That's my deal."

"Deal as long as I make no promises on what I do with said information." I caved, but I needed her. She would manage more analytics and robotics in this project, meaning she had the keys to the IT castle.

The People Team meeting was a hit with our new assignment. Rita sauntered in with her high heels and low blouse, casually pointing in the center of the table of tech employees - all male. They about fell over themselves getting up to get her a chair.

I had silenced my phone during the meeting. I have constant paranoia I'll be the poor soul who's phone blazes an embarrassing ringtone in the middle of a dead silent room of people. I've witnessed that and it's not pretty. When it was finally over, meaning my first day was over, I had messages from Mrs. MacArthur and Milo. *Mrs. MacArthur can birth humans and text. She's such a Rockstar.*

> *Mrs. Jane MacArthur: Eva and Jack have decided on dinner, Italian. I took the liberty of making reservations at a place not too far from home because it's popular and fills up.*

> *Milo: I'm working late tonight. I'll be over after. Midnight maybe.*

I was taking the kids out to a celebratory dinner tonight. I had told them they could choose whatever they wanted, and I was thrilled it wasn't chicken nuggets. Mrs. MacArthur was turning into a lifesaver and I decided to make sure flowers were in her next grocery pickup. I texted her back thank you and told her I was starting the commute home.

Milo's text was presumptuous, but God it was sexy. Coming over at midnight, as tempting as it sounded, seemed like a lot fast. I knew what it meant, and I crossed my legs with a squeeze thinking about him inside me. It seemed desperate though, me waiting up for him to fuck me. Not that I had anything else to do, but still.

That sounds good baby, but I'll probably be asleep.

My phone buzzed before I could get it into my bag.

I have a key.

Oh, shit that's right. It's his house. All the voices in my head screaming YES and NO, back and forth begging me to be bad but praying to be good. They hit me all at once and I had no idea how to respond to him. I loaded myself in the elevator still staring at my phone, undecided.

Rita met me in the lobby after arranging things with our new investigator from the tech group. That woman works fast. She looked at my shaken expression and then my phone. She ripped it from my hands.

After scrolling for a moment her fingers worked quickly and she plopped it in my bag with a wink and started out the doors.

I scrambled after her, digging for my phone, panicked. I gulped when I pulled it out to read the message.

Wake me up and don't be soft about it.

I started typing frantically. What do I say? That was Rita, not me - don't do that. But I wanted him to do that. He texted back before I could compose a retreat.

Go to sleep early. You'll need to rest.

CHAPTER 19

Dear Paul,

I'm not hurt that you weren't at the airport. I'm not hurt that you could never call me or video chat with me. Hell, I'm not even hurt you purposely spaced out letters for years. You did that for your wife. She's what matters most. She's your family.

It's not the way I would like it, and the overall situation does hurt, but your specific actions do not. As usual, you were trying to be everyone for everybody. That's because you are a good person.

Here's the way I see it. You have two options and I support whatever you choose because – well - I care about you. You helped get me through the WORST time in my life. You saved my life. I'm afraid of what I would have done to myself if you hadn't been there. I felt like a murderer. People called me one to my face. Whatever happens, just know that. Tell Claudia that if you think it will help. She should know the amazing man she's married to.

So, option 1 – This is our last letter. It sucks I know, but I repeat -

your wife and your family matter more than anything. I'll always be silently cheering for you to succeed and be happy. I'll be there if you ever need me and decide to reach out. It will be goodbye and that's okay. I'm okay. I took your advice and I'm seeing him, Milo, the guy who I thought may be a stalker. Maybe he is a little - I don't know - but I do still feel that connection with him. I think I'm becoming happy. It's wild I tell you. My point though is I want you to be happy. Whatever that means.

Option 2 – We just keep going like this through a post office box until Claudia comes around and hopefully that's before the next five and a half months. Clock's ticking man. I can't tell you what to do, but I do feel a bit guilty. Like sneaking around but not in a dirty way, but still a bad way. You know what I mean. If you want me to accidentally run into you all somewhere too, I'm totally down. Just tell me in advance if I need to wear a bullet-proof vest or something because that may not qualify for Amazon 1-day shipping.

You know where I am in Winlin because you found the damn house. You are always welcome to come by. Which speaking of, the guy I'm seeing is my landlord technically, I guess. Maybe you know him! Milo Bennett. That's crazy right.

Hearts and stars (and tears and bars)

~Mel

P.S. This is so weird being so close but still a million miles away. I hope you figure it out where this isn't the end, but I get it if I don't hear back from you. Thank you for saving my life.

CHAPTER 20

I mailed the letter on my way out the door with Jack and Eva. I had to do a 3-2-1 countdown before dropping it in the box where it could no longer be clawed out. The situation had hurt me, but not Paul's actions. I didn't think he had made the best choices, but no one knew better than myself what it was like to make impossible choices for those we love. People have an opinion about what they would do if and when, but the truth is most people are cowards. Making a choice is hard. Saying enough is hard. He wasn't ready to let go of our friendship, but he didn't want to lose his wife.

We walked to the Winlin Wag to pick up Trish. I left a standing dinner invite with her for any night of the week and her text came at the perfect time. The reservation was already for four because Mrs. MacArthur didn't know that Rita was out with Robert tonight.

Trish was happy to spend an evening with me and the kids as a surrogate aunt but made me promise to run an extra two miles with her Saturday if she ordered carbohydrates at dinner. When we arrived to pick her up, she started walking out the front door, ready for us. She was wearing a crop tank and high waist jeans. A huge smile spread across her lips as she reached for Jack's hand.

"Will you be my date sir?" she said as his little hand clasped into hers. He beamed up at her excited for another opportunity at pizza. "You will love this place. It's got the best atmosphere and the food and wine are to die for. We can walk so that's always a plus."

"Lead the way," I said ready for the wonderful night. My heart pounded at the thought of my plans after dinner.

Mrs. MacArthur was right about the popularity. People were huddled in groups outside waiting for tables. The entire restaurant had twinkle lights strewn around the outside in rows by the outdoor seating. Servers were scurrying around with entire bottles of wine balancing on their trays. Laughter could be heard from blocks away.

Trish gave a few hugs as she walked up to people she knew. Jack was still on her hand waving high to everyone he met. Eva clung by me taking in the sights with a smile. She seemed so at peace here already - happy to spend her days with Jack and Mrs. MacArthur and excited about school. Mrs. MacArthur had already told me they had a small dance floor and children were welcome to take part.

We sat inside and immediately ordered a bottle of wine, bruschetta, and mozzarella sticks for the kids. It was clear this place had a laid-back atmosphere. No one was in a rush to flip tables, and everyone seemed to know each other. A few people who knew Trish came up to our table. Jack and Eva had made friends with kids at the table next to ours. They shuttled back and forth from the dance floor - snacking through their dinner while

Trish and I sipped wine and talked about life.

We had covered all the basic topics when Trish started in on the real stuff. "I heard you're a widow," she said pouring the last of the bottle in my glass.

"It's been barely two weeks, and everyone already knows that?" I griped.

"Define everyone," Trish said with a smirk. "I just heard you were here for a fresh start. I admire that."

I swirled the wine in my glass thinking seriously about chugging it on the spot. "I am a widow. Eva was barely one. She won't ever know her father."

Trish was completely at ease with the conversation. "How did he die?"

"That's a loaded question."

"Is it?" she quipped, with a puzzled expression.

"It is for what happened with Mitch. There was what killed him, but also how he died." I could feel the lump in my throat begin to form. There was too much alcohol in my bloodstream for this conversation. Tears started to prick my eyes at the memories. The confusion of what happened, and then what I should have done, and what I did.

Trish sat back in her chair and sipped. "You're done with this topic so let's drop it. Are you dating anyone in the states?"

"Um no. I don't do long distance." *That was an excuse and I knew it.*

"So, would you date anyone here? I mean since you might go back. I have a brother, he's a nob, but also hot so I'm told. Yuck - but seriously."

I could feel the redness creep up my chest. I felt like I could trust Trish, and I was dying to tell someone who may know Milo. "I'm kind of dating someone already. It just started but it's gotten intense really fast."

This got her attention. "Here? Who is it?" Her eyes darted back and forth as she considered her question.

Jack and Eva ran up at that inopportune moment. Trish was desperate to start the inquiry but knew better. They ate quickly but seemed settled in their seats for a rest. Eva grabbed my hand and started moving to the music with me at the table. We giggled and Jack clapped to the beat.

The night had been filled with laughing and dancing, sipping wine. I was ready to talk to Trish about Milo, but I would have to park it for the moment.

I had felt comfortable the entire night, but an uneasiness had started to creep into my spine. Maybe it was her questions about Mitch, but I had filtered those types of things a million times before. This was more, this was intuition.

"I need to pop to the ladies," I said standing to excuse myself. Trish nodded and signaled a circle over the table with her hand which meant she would keep an eye on the kids.

My breath felt shallow as I started across the restaurant. I walked slowly and steadily scanning the room. Maybe it was the wine or dancing on top of a huge day in my new life. Too much excitement and anticipation for what was to come.

I hadn't realized I was at a standstill in an aisle until a server had to gently nudge me to one side. I stepped to the left but didn't move my gaze. I had been staring at a table to the front of the restaurant tucked in the corner away from the dancefloor. There were four men seated and two were clearly arguing. One of the men in the discussion looked so angered I was sure he was withholding punches because he was in a public place. I could see his face tense with frustration. He shook his head and pointed his finger in the other man's face. I could only see the back of his opponent, but I knew who it was.

I knew it was Milo he was cursing under his breath.

In the same way, I knew something was off in this place they sensed me watching. The man who a moment ago appeared livid now had a shocked expression. He made eye contact with me and I took a few steps forward.

Milo turned, and seeing me, raised from his chair so fast it tipped over.

He marched over, taking my hands and placing them on his chest. "Who is that man," I asked. I knew him, but I couldn't place him. The expression he had was forlorn, almost sad.

"That's my brother," Milo said. "We are talking about business. You shouldn't be here."

It took a moment for what he said to register, but when it did - I was pissed. "I shouldn't be here," I said. "This is a restaurant walking distance from my house. You can't tell me where I can be."

"Yes, you are right. I just - we are just - we aren't having a great dinner. I didn't want you to meet my family like this." He started to edge me to the wall of the restaurant. He still had my hands on his chest as he walked, and we were stepping through the side door as I gave his table a last look.

"I'm not having dinner by myself you know," I said reaching back for the door. "I can't just go outside."

"Who are you having dinner with," Milo said with a wary tone. He was concerned I was here with a man. I could tell by the fire that flickered in his eyes.

"Trish and the kids. Now, what the hell is going on? You said you were working and now you are down the street arguing with your brothers trying to push me as far away as possible."

Milo hung his head and kissed the palms of my hands. "It's just become a crazy night. I'm sorry."

It occurred to me that maybe he was embarrassed by me. The American renting his home was easy prey. His brothers were already upset about whatever business they had together. You add in that he's messing around with a single mom and they may beat him up if they were true British gentlemen. He whisked me away and didn't introduce me. Shit, we were outside.

I'm so stupid.

I began to feel the familiar lump rise in my throat. "I'm going back in through the front."

Milo gripped my hands tighter, "I just wanted a moment with you. Look at me. Kiss me."

He cupped my face in his hands and softly brushed my lips with his. I responded despite myself. I couldn't help it. All of me wanted him, but as the intensity grew in our embrace, I placed my hand on his chest and pushed away. He pulled against me tighter fighting my push. "Don't," he said. "Don't pull away. I need you."

"She wants you to stop Milo." One of his brothers had come outside and was standing inches away from us. He was almost the same height as Milo and the resemblance was there. Same dark hair. Same broad chest. Same brooding anger bubbling up in his face. His fists clenched by his sides and his voice was almost shaking.

Milo turned and faced him chest to chest. "This isn't your business. Do not do this." The look between them was unreadable. A mix of anger and sadness, maybe. *What were they arguing about?*

"Well I'm Mel," I interjected in an attempt to ease the tension. They both shot their gaze to me. "You know if anyone is interested or wants to introduce me."

"I know who you are," his brother said to me. His rage was gone when he spoke to me. His face turned kind and he reached out, but not to shake my hand – to embrace me.

Milo grabbed his forearm and yanked it down. "Don't touch her. We're leaving." He grabbed my hand and started walking to the front of the restaurant. I looked back at his brother who stood with a lost expression on his face.

What the hell is going on?

"I'm not leaving with you," I said. He kept walking and pushed through the front doors. "Did you hear me? I'm not leaving, and you aren't coming over tonight." At that - he stopped and turned to me. We were close to my table and I could see Trish's jaw drop. "This has gone from zero to nine thousand. We need to pause."

His expression deflated. "I'll explain soon. Please don't pull away from me."

We had just met, but he felt the same way I did. We were brought together in some way by something, but I kept my resolve. We needed to breathe for a moment. I needed to think. I needed Rita's background check for one.

"You need to work things out with your brother tonight. Focus on your family."

"No," he yelled gripping my hand tight to him.

"Yes," I ripped away and hauled it towards Trish. She had picked up the vibe and started collecting our things.

"Hey sorry to rush out," I told her.

"I need a full debrief on the way home," she responded in a hush. Milo trailed behind me and stilled when he reached us. He grabbed his wallet pulled out a wad of cash and threw it on the table saying nothing. He was pissed. *He looked hot when he was pissed.*

"I won't force you, but I'll be waiting," he said and walked away.

Once I had put the kids to bed, I called Trish. She could hardly hold in her questions on the way home. I texted Rita that I would keep Jack and Eva because they were exhausted from dancing the night away and she promised to owe me one.

I didn't tell Trish very much, just that he was the new potential guy I was dating. I was more interested in what she might know about him and the mysterious brother that he was fighting with.

Trish had grown up with Milo, but she wasn't forthcoming with a lot of details. I could tell she knew more, but I was a new friend to her and Milo was an old friend. Her allegiance was clear.

She did give me some information. He had moved away several years ago and only recently moved back. There was family drama that I had witnessed firsthand. She seemed shocked he was pursuing me, but not because it was me. She seemed surprised he was interested in anyone. She used the words loner and independent a lot. Too exhausted to continue a conversation that was going nowhere, I ended the call with not much more than I started with.

When I heard Milo's footsteps in the foyer, my breath caught.

Would he push in?

At that moment I didn't know if I wanted him to, but if he did, I wouldn't be able to stop myself. I could hear my shallow breath as I waited. He was outside my door. I hadn't heard him open and shut his yet. Moments passed and then – the front door to the duplex slammed. He didn't come to see me and he didn't go home.

My phone buzzed.

Goodnight Mel. Say when.

CHAPTER 21

I had spent my entire weekend trying to process everything with Milo. Trish and I ran five miles Saturday. It didn't help my pent-up energy. Rita and I talked nonstop about it and she didn't seem to ever get sick of the topic. Her advice continued to be that I needed to "get on that dick" - direct quote.

I never saw him or heard him in the house. There had not been a peep on the other side of the wall. Monday he was nowhere on our way to work and Rita held my hand while I sniffled. Pitiful as it was.

I had told Paul he could go away.

I had pushed Milo away.

Alone again.

Work was ramping up and I thankfully didn't have time to dwell on the men in my life during our hectic days. I barely had time to shove a free bagel in my mouth from the breakfast bar. My confusion about my personal life created the need for consistency somewhere - and that somewhere was work.

I stayed late at the office every night that Rita had the kids. I had to use a corporate car to get home. I would arrive at an empty house on my side and his, so why not be productive. We were already on day seventeen of the projected timeline. If others fell behind, I had picked up the slack. Rita didn't dare question my tenacity. She knew I needed this. I needed to win at something - be sure of something - and she had her fair share of late nights keeping up.

I was completely engrossed in the project plan Friday when Rita stormed into my office and slammed her hands on my desk with full force. I jolted back in my chair as she stood at attention. She beamed like the cat that got the cream.

"I got all the dirt," she said and started digging a manilla folder out of her bag.

"What?" I said confused.

"Milo Bennett. I got a deep dive. Paul we are still working on. Are you sure his name is Paul Masterson? Do you have a date of birth or anything?"

"Yes, I'm sure and no I don't." *But was I?* I didn't know he was hiding our friendship, or that his wife secretly hated me. I didn't have a letter back yet and I doubted that I would.

"Anyway, take a look." Rita handed the file over and scurried to my side of the desk. She moved my stack of papers to the side and sat next to the file.

"Are you going to read this with me?" I asked looking up at her. Hypocritical, I knew, that I wanted privacy while invading his privacy. "I don't see why this even matters. I haven't figured out if I can handle him." *Even though I still wanted him.*

"Oh, I've already read it." She shrugged. "Sorry, not sorry. I'll give you some highlights. He's loaded. Never married. He's been to America once."

"Okay let me just look," I said holding up my hand.

I opened the file to see a top sheet of Milo Bennett's picture. He wasn't facing the camera and looked ahead walking on a street in the shot. A few days stubble lined his chin and he wore his usual solid shirt and jeans. I could see the lines of his collar bone and chest hair in the opening of his T-shirt. He may have been a bit disheveled but still so handsome. *When was this taken?*

There was all the standard information in the beginning. Date of birth, previous addresses, family history. Three brothers I knew, father in senior living, check. Maybe I could get to know him just by being with him. This could be overkill.

Business holdings included Winlin Investments. I started to read down the rental properties. He didn't own just our home. He owned the whole damn town. He owned the Winlin Wag and six other restaurants. He and his brothers that is.

"I thought that would catch your attention," Rita said. "Let's go to the residence history page." She flipped through the file and pointed her polished nail at his previous addresses. In the past ten years, he had only moved three times. And then I saw it. Change of address one month ago to 41 Winlin Ave.

"Why would someone worth millions move to a duplex two weeks before I arrived," I mumbled.

"EXACTLY," Rita said slamming her hand on the page. "Exactly the question you should ask him when you see him. Tonight."

CHAPTER 22

Before I could object, Rita had my phone in her hand, unlocked. She cocked an eyebrow moving the phone back and forth in my face. I motioned for her to continue. I wouldn't have the guts to text Milo, but I knew it had to be done.

I should be scared at this moment. I should run from Milo. Instead, I felt more desperate to find out the truth. I had missed him terribly through the week, keeping myself so occupied I didn't have to think about him. The nights were still long and miserable. I cried in my bed instead of sleeping, knowing that he wasn't on the other side of the wall. I dreamt of his touch and would wake up aching for him.

Touching myself was a pathetic excuse for a solution and I could never get far without giving up and falling into my misery. Lying in bed thinking of his hands gave me more pleasure than my own. I needed him.

Rita handed the phone back to me.

Hi – I need to see you this weekend.

I'll come over tonight. 9?

That had been quick. He must have been waiting for me. A man that does what he says. The typing bubbles started to appear and I pulled the phone closer to me. Rita stood away from my desk and announced we were leaving early and going shopping.

I tried to resist her invitation with an excuse, but she reminded me we could take a week off work and still be ahead on the project, so I needed to get my shit. My phone pinged.

I may be closer to 10. Dinner with my brothers.

He was telling me what he was doing this time. His brothers weren't my main concern anymore, but there was a mystery there too. I collected my bag and followed her out. I had already logged maybe seventy hours this week. It was time for the weekend.

"What are we shopping for?" I asked Rita as we headed into a crowded elevator.

"Lingerie," she boasted.

A few heads turned around and one man coughed. I didn't even flinch anymore. I was used to Rita embarrassing me all over England now. If blunt, uncomfortable commentary was a sport, she had the gold medal.

"I hope this is for Robert's return," I whispered harshly to her.

She lifted her hands to her hips, exasperated. "Are you new here, Mel? You can try to fight it, but I'm buying you some sexy shit." We exited the elevator much to the relief of others. Rita seemed certain of where she was going as we left the building and I followed.

"You aren't concerned that Milo is some crazy stalker? This doesn't seem at all odd to you? Shouldn't you be telling me to run the other way instead of trying to sex me up?"

"I have my thoughts and predictions," she said with a wink. "This is the first man you have been interested in since Mitch died. That deserves new panties. You want to make him suffer for being a stalker, new panties. You want to bang him all night, new panties. It's a win-win."

"What are your predictions?" I said stopping on the street. A woman almost ran into me from behind and she audibly groaned as she pushed by me.

Rita reached her hand out for mine. She sighed as we hooked arms and started walking again. "Mel, this guy - this feeling you have where you are linked to him - that hunch comes from somewhere. Maybe he sought you out, but how bad is that really?"

"None of those are answers, woman."

Another exhale from her as we marched down the street. "I don't have a specific answer. He's not a danger to you. Let's go inside."

She let go and started into the store. I was sure she wasn't telling me everything. I looked in my bag at the manilla folder she had given me. I would go through it tonight before Milo came over. Maybe my answer was in there.

When I entered the shop, a young woman dressed in a black knee-length dress greeted me with champagne. She offered a raspberry for my glass and I accepted. Rita had her own glass and she was walking along the shop walls, lightly touching the garments.

This place screamed expensive, but I could afford it. The pay bump coming here combined with the housing and per diem budget already left me with a huge surplus on my first check today. I hadn't calculated the increase fully and was pleasantly surprised.

The store had soft lighting and classical music which gave an elegance to the silk robes and lace bras. There were no price tags which told me I was right about emptying my wallet a bit. A woman came out from behind the counter. She was also dressed in black, but her lips were bright red.

"Hello, I'm Emma," she said as she smiled, assessing our attire. We were dressed as business professionals and Rita was wearing Louboutin's, so we passed inspection. "You are welcome to peruse the store, however, we find that an assessment of what you are looking for paired with some measurements allows us to shop for our clients. Our results are impeccable."

Cha-ching, Cha-ching, Cha-ching

Rita met her gaze. "We would like a room together. Please show the way."

Emma eyed us both and then started towards the back of the store.

"Great now she thinks we are lesbians," I hissed to Rita.

"And I give a fuck why?" she said. True, if we were spending a hundred pounds for a pair of panties, this woman could think whatever she wanted. A sale is a sale.

I had never had so much attention paid to me even when being measured and fitted for my wedding dress. Two women surrounded me as I stood on a small podium in a dark room. Since I was topless, I was happy to have dim lighting. Rita sipped her second glass of champagne and surfed her phone.

One woman carried a measuring tape around her neck. She would pull on one end to take measurements of my chest, back, arms, and who knew what else. She quickly jotted numbers in a small notepad, completely focused on her assignment.

The other asked questions that would normally make me blush all over, but her tone and demeanor were comforting. She had a calming quality that was almost hypnotic.

Are you looking for a one-use outfit, day to day wear, or both? Would you like to wear your ensemble during your encounters, or have it removed? What do you consider the most beautiful part of your body? What do you consider the most erotic part of your body?

Rita traded places with me going through the same process. She was more assertive with her answers, which wasn't surprising.

They took an order for a late lunch - fruit, sandwiches, and croissants. We sat on the couch, wrapped in silk robes, as they reviewed their notes then left the room. Whatever would happen with Milo tonight or in the future, it was wonderful to have someone give me individual attention.

"This is nice," I said to Rita sinking into the couch. "I should listen to you more often."

"Say it again," Rita chuckled. "I could get used to that."

We chatted a little about Robert. I had never seen Rita so happy. She told me that it didn't matter what they brought in for her to wear, that Robert would love it. He adored everything about her and told her often. She was always confident, but now she was comfortable as well. To have a man admiring you head to toe - every day - was something that I had forgotten since Mitch.

A clothing rack with silk hangers that had more fabric than the garments they held pushed into the room. Each piece was intricately made with precision and care. I had never seen anything like it, and for the first time, I understood the cost assigned to things like this.

Rita stood and pointed to an emerald green teddy. Emma seemed pleased that she was drawn to it and remarked how it was her pick for Rita's coloring and desired aesthetic. As she tried it on, I felt a pang of fear. I wouldn't look like Rita standing on the pedestal in the dressing room. She oozed confidence and sex appeal. Every curve of her was perfect. She could cause a heart attack in that get-up.

Emma brought over a burgundy bra and panty set and gestured for me to stand up. It was a silk overlay with lace trimming on the bra. The thong was silk and had lace on the sides where the band would graze my hip. There was a crisscross pattern on both with thin strands for the front and back. It was gorgeous on the hanger and I hoped it would look half as good on me.

"Our items are not resold after they are tried on," Emma said sensing my hesitation. "Although I can't recall a time a woman didn't go home in what we choose for her." There was a silk curtain on the side of the room and I carefully slipped into the set from behind it. Emma had been right in her choice and now I didn't think I could buy panties like a normal human again. I felt like a goddess in the set and when I stepped out to see myself in the mirror, Rita's expression confirmed my thoughts. I didn't even look at the receipt. It was worth every penny to have the confidence tonight when I saw Milo.

Rita had accomplished her mission. We had an early Friday with some much-needed girlfriend time. It was everything I needed at this moment. I was anxious to get home and comb through Milo's file, but time was not on my side. When we made it to Mrs. MacArthur's, chatted a bit, fed the kids, and got all their things to Rita's, it was after eight. I still needed a shower and a gallon of wine.

When I finally felt settled, it was nine and I barely had time to skim the file. Milo had a key, but I wasn't sure if he would use it.

He had purchased his first rental property at nineteen. A year later, another, and then the next year he had purchased three. There weren't any bank affiliations, so I could only assume it was a snowball cash deal. Making money on one and then using it to fund the others.

No news articles, arrests, or marriages. *Okay so maybe I'm the first stalking victim.*

There were a few pages on his brothers. Two were married and had children. There was a picture of the four of them with a post-it attached. Left to right, Maxwell, Marcus, Milo, and Marshall. It had been Marshall screaming at Milo last week. They all seemed to follow in Milo's footsteps. They were added to the limited liability companies only after Milo had created the entities.

When I reached the end of the file, it was after ten and Milo hadn't come to either side of the home yet. I felt a small twinge of dread. *What if he didn't show?*

I properly hid the file in my closet and just as I exited my bedroom, I heard my phone ping.

I'm outside your door

I set the phone down in the kitchen and turned the ringer off. I didn't want any distractions. My heart thudded in my chest and I walked toward the door, clicking the lock and pausing with my fingers on the handle. I felt the knob turn under my palm as Milo pushed in. He stepped through my doorway hurriedly. Without as much as a hello, his mouth was on mine.

"I missed you," he said as he broke from our kiss. He set his forehead to mine and, for a moment, I had forgotten all the questions I had lined up for him. Gaining my senses, I stepped back and started towards the kitchen.

"I have a kettle now like a proper English person," I said with a chuckle. "Would you like some tea?"

Milo set his keys on my end table. He was wearing his familiar boots, jeans, and a white shirt. I could see every muscle from underneath. He exhaled as he sat at the table. He knew I wanted to talk. I knew he did not.

I was painfully aware of what I was wearing under my black tank top and jeans. I had to resist the urge to go back, keep kissing, and show him.

"Do Americans like tea?" he asked stretching out in a chair.

"Not this American," I quipped back. "But I also have wine. Red or White."

"Whatever is open." He pulled out the chair next to him making sure I would sit at his side and not across the table. There was a fire in his eyes, and why wouldn't there be? He was over here at ten at night. I could feel him staring at me as I rummaged through the fridge.

"Is Eva home?"

Nothing was open so I grabbed a bottle of red set it on the counter and started the corkscrew. "She's at Rita's. We promised the kids sleepovers until school starts."

He smiled at that comment. "How was your week?"

I sat the wine glasses on the table and looked at him deadpan. "It wasn't great," I said.

"Mine was terrible. I missed you," he said adding a hefty pour to our glasses.

"You never came home. Where did you go?"

"My brother's. Not the angry one." Milo looked down as he continued. "I wouldn't have been able to stay away from you here. I would have come over. Or I would have tried." He held my forearm with his hand and moved up to my shoulder, gently rubbing along the way. I didn't pull away.

"What is happening with your brothers? Did you work things out with your family?" I asked calmly.

Milo released my shoulder and sat back in his chair. His chest rose and fell with every breath as I waited for his answer. I bit my tongue. I wasn't going to babble and give myself away.

"No," he said. "And it's only one brother. The others remain......unbiased."

I stayed silent and watched him. He shifted in his chair uncomfortably, knowing that answer would elicit more questions.

"Marshall does not agree with me pursuing you," he said. I stiffened, but I maintained my composure. Reacting wouldn't help anyone.

It was my turn to talk though. "So, you have a friend who didn't want you to move here? And your brother is upset you want to - whatever it is you want to do with me?" That did not seem like a good start even if you were the most optimistic of women.

"They are one and the same. I argued with my brother the day you arrived."

"Are you embarrassed that we, you know? Am I not what they would approve of?" I asked as I felt the red creep up my neck.

His hands moved to grab mine, but I kept them firmly placed on my knees.

"What I want is to be with you," he said. "In every way that you can imagine. I'm not embarrassed. I'm private. Marshall has a lot of ideas about what I should and shouldn't be doing. He's always been like that. He's in an unhappy marriage, and it bleeds over us all. Max and me more than the others because we're unmarried. It has nothing to do with who you are - which by the way is perfection."

My cheeks flushed and I had to focus on breathing at a normal pace. "Why is this moving so fast?" I asked looking him in the eye. "Is it because I'm only here for a few months?"

"It's because when I want something, I get it. Why waste time and play games? You should know life is too short for that."

"I keep getting reminded - yes."

"This is slow for me. You would have been in my bed a week ago if I had it my way. We wouldn't have spent a night apart. If you want to wait on that because of Eva, I understand. But don't misunderstand my intentions. I want you and no matter what my brother says or does - I'll have you."

"What he does? What would he do?" I sputtered, leaning towards him.

Before Milo could answer, his mouth was back on mine. He moved his hands up to my shoulders and one wrapped around the back of my neck. He stood up, kissing me from above. Our kiss was deep and slow. I had more questions, but my resolve was waning. We had all night. My body had made that decision the moment I saw him.

He pulled on the back of my neck, standing, and I rose to my feet with him. In one quick motion, I was lifted, my legs wrapped around him as he started walking out of the kitchen. I knew where we were going. I knew I would be on my back in a moment, but I didn't stop him. We kept kissing as he used his free hand to guide him along the walls.

He lowered me on the bed hovering over me. "Tell me you want me, Mel. Tell me yes. I won't force you." I trembled beneath him as he spoke. He raised his body slightly, grabbed his shirt from behind his neck, and pulled it off over his head. I reached out and touched his chiseled chest with my fingertips tracing them lower until they rested on the top of his belt buckle.

"Yes," I said in a barely audible whisper. My hand stayed frozen in its place. I could not stop shaking from underneath him.

Our eyes stayed locked as he spoke. "Unbuckle it." I shifted my gaze down and lifted my other hand to his waist. I obeyed and pulled the belt out from each loop and it clicked through one at a time while my hands shook. He took my palm and kissed it and then placed it on his length. He was rock hard and pulsing. My breath caught as he moved his hands to my jeans.

Slowly he undid the top button and slid the zipper down. He moved to his jeans, unbuttoning and unzipping, and then stepped back off the bed. Gripping my belt loops, he pulled as I arched upward. He threw them in a pile on the floor, lowered his jeans, and kicked them back to the same spot. I lifted my shirt over my head as I waited for him. I could see the tip of him from the top of his boxer briefs and my breath caught.

His back stiffened and eyes widened. He stood at the edge of the bed - taking me in. Despite my best efforts, I was losing my confidence under his steady gaze. I started to raise my arms to cover myself. "Don't," he growled and ran his hand down from my clavicle to my hips rubbing his thumb over the delicate fabric. "Beautiful," he whispered with heavy eyes.

I blushed and fidgeted until he crawled back onto the bed and rested his elbows on either side of me. I could feel his heat beating down in waves.

"Tell me you need it," he whispered in my ear. I panted from underneath him. "I need to know you want me. It's me you need inside you. Carmela, please."

His last statement seemed almost desperate. I was quivering uncontrollably underneath him. He had to know I was eager for him. He had to know by the way I was reacting to him, but he wanted to hear it. The words had to leave my chest. He was removing his boxer briefs now with one hand. I could feel him spring free on the inside of my thigh. He didn't push forward, didn't kiss me, he was waiting.

He reached behind my back and unhooked my bra, dragging the straps down my arms, still balanced above me. I curved my back as he removed the fabric from my hips and then I heard it land in the pile of clothes on the floor. I reached my hands to his face. This was the first time I genuinely wanted a man in six years. *Tell him, Mel.*

"Milo," I said almost a croak. I swallowed my anxiety and started again. "Milo, I need you inside me. I need you now, and don't hold back."

With that he positioned himself, lowered to kiss me, and entered me in one motion. I gasped and bowed my back as he filled me. The satisfaction spread heat through my entire body.

"Are you okay?" he asked breathlessly. I nodded, and he rocked himself out and in again, this time deeper. He moaned and shifted back and forth again, and again, finding his rhythm. His chin was tight, and his shoulders were raised. I could tell he was concentrating on not hurting me, being careful.

"I said don't hold back," I gasped. "I meant it."

The fire in his eyes intensified and his jaw went slack. He lifted his torso and yanked me towards him by my hips. Pulling my legs over his shoulders he pumped harder and faster. My thighs rested against his chest and he held them in place with one arm, reaching down with the other cupping my breasts.

He rolled my nipple between his fingers, and I cried out from the sensation. I wanted him this way. Ruthless and intense - grunting with every shove. He could make love to me later - right now I needed him to fuck me.

As his thrusts continued, I felt the warmth rise in myself. I began to writhe underneath him and whimper. I moved my nails into his sides and thrashed my body to get him as deep as possible. He could tell I was close and moved his thumb down my stomach and pressed it to my clit.

"Oh God Milo," I muttered. I was already coming completely undone. He knew how to touch me and followed my reactions to all the right spots.

"Yes baby," he said. "Tell me you need me." His eyes met mine with such passion I would have said anything at that moment.

"I need you," I cried. My release began making my thighs shake uncontrollably. I kept repeating it over and over as the wave of pleasure moved through my entire body.

I need you, I need you, I need you.

When I reached the peak I tensed and shuddered, clamping down hard on him screaming his name. I was covered in sweat, my heart thudding through my chest, and a limp mess of a woman as my body began to relax. Everything tingled and I could barely move.

Milo continued unshaken. He never slowed slamming into me with focus. His body was tensed and had a sheen of sweat over his perfectly sculpted chest. I could hear his heavy breathing as I lay with hooded eyes letting him have what was left of me.

He moved my legs down around his waist and wrapped his arms behind my back lifting me into his lap, chest to chest. My arms draped around his neck and I laid my head on his shoulder trying to match his movements with what little energy I had left.

"I'm on birth control," I said.

He turned his face to mine. "I would be coming inside you either way," he said pushing and pulling my hips with his hands. His eyes started to squint as his mouth opened slightly. I could feel him swell inside me.

I held him tightly and barely touched my lips to his. Something in this man had to be reminded, had to be told, that I desired him. How could someone so gorgeous and so successful need that reassurance?

"I need you, Milo," I breathed into his ear.

With that, his hands clutched my hips as he slammed me hard onto him one last time. His chest vibrated with a deep groan as he poured himself into me. I could feel his pulse inside and outside my body.

I didn't know it could be like this. Not since Mitch. I didn't know I could be so sated and full of pleasure.

His grip was around me so tight that I had to concentrate on breathing. We sat there like that until our heartbeats slowed. I was close to sleep when he laid me on my side, kissing me from my shoulders to my hips. It made me feel cared for - maybe even loved.

I drifted into a sound sleep when he climbed into bed next to me. He was staying, he wanted me, and he needed me. I needed the rest, and we could finish our talk in the morning. I snuggled into his chest and relaxed as he gently rubbed my back.

I was in the same position when I awoke at three in the morning. My eyes opened when I realized it wasn't a dream. We hadn't moved when the knocking became banging. I felt Milo's squeeze on me grow tighter as I lifted to see who was there. His eyes were wide open and glared at the ceiling.

"Where's my phone? It could be Rita. It could be Eva!" I said trying to move from his arm.

He turned and pinned me to the bed. "I know exactly who it is Mel. Stay here."

CHAPTER 23

Milo rose from the bed with clenched fists. He looked down at me and attempted a smile.

"Don't worry, baby," he spoke with all the calmness he could manage - which wasn't much. "I'll take care of this. Everything is fine."

He rose pulling the curtain back for some moonlight to find his clothes. I sat up in bed pulling the comforter over my naked body, my heart beating out of my chest. My phone wasn't in my room. Shit.

Bang. Bang. Bang.

He pulled his jeans on and started out my bedroom door as he buttoned. His back muscles were clenched tight when he walked out. He was livid and I was scared.

Bang. Bang. Bang.

I heard Milo yell, "Stop!" My bedroom door was shut and I scrambled to it, turning the lock. I scavenged the room for my clothes and then realized this was my room and I should just put on fresh clothes that didn't have my nervous sex sweat all over them. My brain wasn't problem-solving in the early hours of the morning with a stranger banging on my door.

After locating some yoga pants and a T-shirt I crouched on the other side of the door. I placed my ear on the door and strained to listen. I could hear Milo's voice but couldn't make out any words. He was too far away, still at my front door maybe. The other voice was male – louder British accent - but still, I couldn't tell.

Dammit. I would have to go out there.

I released the lock as softly as I could and turned the handle, pulling the door open an inch at a time so I wouldn't make any noise. I realized he had to be at the front of the house. I could see my kitchen and living room, but not that far down the hall. I couldn't see my phone either. I looked back in the room to scan it for Milo's. I knew Rita's number and could use his if it was unlocked, but nothing. I recalled he had his hands full when we got in the bedroom, so it was likely both phones were elsewhere in the house.

I slid out of the door and stayed close to the wall. With every step, I strained to hear the conversation. Milo was sure of who it was which eased my nerves a bit. Knowing him, he wouldn't tell me much if I didn't hear it on my own. We had barely scratched the surface of my questions.

I was at the corner of my bedroom hall and the wall to the living area. This was as close as I could get without being seen. I closed my eyes and stilled my breath to hear. There were only a few words I could make out and then I heard my name. I stretched my neck a bit, and there it was again. They were talking about me.

I had to risk it and step out there. I would never hear the entire conversation this way. Headfirst, I stepped out into the living room. Milo's bare back was to me, shadowing the view of the other man. Hushed angry whispers filled the space between them. I hadn't been noticed yet.

I walked forward and Milo's brother came into view. The one from the restaurant. I was sure of who it was now.

"Marshall," I said as I stepped forward. They both stopped and turned to face me. Milo looked dejected. His shoulders hung low and he couldn't bring his eyes to mine. I continued toward them. "I'm guessing you are Marshall. We met for a moment before, but I'm Carmela. Everyone calls me Mel."

Marshall reached for my hand. His expression was unreadable. "Hi, Mel. Nice to finally meet you." Milo stiffened.

Finally?

"Care to tell me why you are banging on my door at this hour," I said unsmiling.

Marshall shifted his hands in his pockets and rocked back on his heels. "I found out in the middle of the night that he came here. So, the middle of the night is when I'm here."

"You get that makes zero sense right," I said letting out a frustrated sigh. Milo reached for my hand and held it tightly.

I continued with Marshall. "What do you mean by finally? Why would there be such an urgency to come over here the second you knew. This is your brother. Maybe you don't approve, but why are you doing this to him? He's obviously upset."

"Mel, it should not have gotten this far. Not near this far. I've known about you, but Milo said he would stay away. He wasn't supposed to even live here."

Milo growled at that, "This is my house. I'll live here if I want to. I shouldn't have told you I was moving here. You never noticed where I was before. It's just because you want what you can't have." Milo grabbed his shirt collar and started to shove him out, but Marshall was equally strong. He broke free and burst past him into the living room.

"I didn't want to do things this way, but you won't hear reason, Milo. You had the opportunity and now what have you done? You made everything worse." Marshall grabbed a wad of paper in a rubber band from his inside jacket pocket. He shook it at Milo's face and continued. "You took advantage of the situation. You did this to me, to us."

Marshall pointed at me as he said us, not his brother. Milo lunged for the papers, but Marshall diverted and pushed them into my hand. "Look at them," he said to me. Marshall had tears filling his eyes, his cheeks were flushed. He was handsome like Milo, so much more so now that he was vulnerable.

I held the papers and watched him. His eyes were pleading, and he touched the side of my face with his other hand. His thumb rubbing the side of my cheek as he pushed the papers forward. "Look."

Boom.

Milo had punched the hallway wall leaving a hole. A picture fell and the glass shattered. Marshall and I both jumped. I wanted to go to him, but I unfolded the papers instead.

Letters.

So many letters.

From me.

To Paul.

May 4th, 1999, Dear Paul, Do you have a homecoming dance in England?

July 4th, 2004, Dear Paul, It's Independence Day. Suck it England.

September 17th, 2007, Dear Paul, I lost my job today. I'm crying on the pages. I don't even know what I did wrong.

January 30th, 2012, Dear Paul, New Years Resolution BUSTED. Every damn year man.

October 3rd, 2014, Dear Paul, I did it today. Everyone hates me. I hate me. It should have been me. Eva deserves better. No one will look at me. Am I a murderer? Am I selfish?

My breathing quickened. The papers started to fall at my feet. The last one in my hand had broken me. My confession to Paul with my worst fears right there in ink. Memories flooded of sitting in my kitchen writing those words thinking about killing myself. Thinking about how I would do it. Who would care? One of the worst days of my life and Marshall was handing me the proof.

"What the fuck is this?" I screamed. "What sick game are you playing?"

Marshall grabbed my shoulders. "This is no game. Milo should have let you be. I was going to get Claudia to understand, but that doesn't matter now. I just needed time. I'm Paul, Mel. Marshall Paul Masterson. I'm Paul. Milo is my half-brother."

Milo ripped him away from me so hard I thought Marshall's arm would rip off. *Or was it Paul's arm?* "You haven't written to her in years," he said. "It's too late."

My tears fell down my cheeks like a river. Nothing was making sense. The floor felt unsteady underneath my feet. Embarrassment and sadness filled my body until I was bawling in a crumpled pile on the floor. They had played me. This was a game for them.

Milo fell to his knees in front of me and put my face in his hands. I tried to resist him with everything in me. Pushing his hands away and shaking my head back and forth. He growled at me, "I've loved you for ten years, Mel. I've been the one writing to you. I need you and you need me. I was going to tell you. Please."

"GET OUT!" I screamed at him, at them both. "Get out of my house. NOW!" I was screaming at the top of my lungs now. I flung my hands and arms at his body pushing him as hard as I could. "LEAVE!"

Marshall took his elbow and Milo shook it away. "Please," Milo said his voice cracking. "If I stay, I can explain. You'll understand. I love you."

I laid on the floor on top of all the letters. I was broken. A woman cannot keep going from the highest highs to the lowest lows - the joy of having a man that loves her and wants her, to hurt, betrayal, and fear.

Again.

I can't do it again.

This is why people don't try. This is why love is a joke.

I didn't sit up. I didn't face them.

"Get out," I bawled. "I don't even know you."

CHAPTER 24

I never fell back asleep on the floor of my house, but I didn't get up until well after sunrise. I heard my phone vibrating somewhere in my kitchen. At first, it was constant, one call after the other. Texts in between. At some point when the sun came up, the sounds lessoned.

No sounds came from Milo's side of the house. Marshall had dragged him out. His large shoulders bumping into the doorframes as they scuffled again in the foyer. Milo had spit at him telling him he wouldn't be happy unless everyone around him was as miserable as he was. Then nothing but the slam of the door.

It's Paul, not Marshall. It's Paul.

Rita had the kids until after lunch, but I needed another night. At some point, I would crash from lack of sleep. I dragged myself into the shower and avoided my phone. The hot water beat on my skin until it was red. I choked on the steam and cried again.

As I stood in front of the mirror, I remembered the girl who looked back. She was in a hole of depression. She hated herself. She had a baby screaming in the other room who she refused to hold. She had food in the kitchen people brought that she never ate to punish herself. She was someone I swore would never return. I loathed everything about her.

"Enough," I said to myself. I dried my hair for as long as I could stand the heat. My entire room was muggy and hot. I threw on some leggings and a tank top. I needed to face my phone.

Cool air hit me as I stepped out of my room. Then Trish's voice hit me and I about jumped out of my skin.

"Well you are up and showered so maybe it wasn't that bad," she said rising from the couch.

Shit. I'm supposed to run with her this morning.

"Milo called," she said. She came up to me and hugged me. It took ninja focus, but I did not cry.

"Did he tell you what happened?" I asked and headed to the kitchen. I needed to fiddle while we talked. I started with the kettle and grabbed a French Press to start some coffee. My phone caught my eye on the table. Thirty-two missed calls. Sixteen messages. *Jesus.*

"I can't say if he did or not. I mean he said a lot." She widened her eyes and sat at my table. When she looked at my phone, she let out a groan.

I started the water in the kettle then walked to my phone in a huff. Rita had called and then texted never mind she would call me later. An unknown number had called a few times then left a message. The rest was Milo. His texts were all simple and to the point, just like him. Shut up Mel you don't even know him.

I scanned the messages.

Please call

I can explain

I'm sorry

I love you

I texted Rita.

> *Hey, I promise I'll explain later but can you have the kids tonight? Tell Eva I love her.*

"Why don't you start with what he said," I snapped as I sat a mug in front of Trish. "Coffee or tea."

"Tea. Whatever you have." Trish sat at attention and cleared her throat. "He called this morning and asked if I was working breakfast. I said no I run with you on Saturdays. He said that was good because he wanted me to check on you. He said he messed things up last night. He had a lot to explain to you about his past and he stalled too long. He wouldn't tell me what - and Mel - I really tried to find out. Sorry. He said his brother took it upon himself to tell you and you kicked him out. He sounded horrible. The worst I've ever heard him."

"Oh, I bet he did," I barked. "Don't cheaters and wife beaters always sound so sad right after?"

"You can't be comparing Milo to a cheater and a wife-beater."

"No - I'm just making a point. People - men actually - are always so sad after they get caught. And then they are absolved like nothing ever happened. Everyone expects the wife to work through it and forgive."

Trish put her elbows on the table and rested her chin in her hands. "What? What are we talking about? Milo or someone else?"

I grabbed a tin of tea and started to smack the bags on the counter. "Earl Grey, Green Tea, or what?"

Trish stared at me deadpan.

"What?" I snapped. She had seen the chink in my armor. She could tell the woman I used to be was peeking through. Her anger was apparent, and I felt it in my chest. I took a deep breath in through my nose and out through my mouth. "I just need a minute."

I stepped into my bedroom to collect myself. I closed my eyes and pictured the best way this day could end. *Fuck that - this day was going to be shit.* How about this morning? What would be the best way this morning would end? I would tell Trish what was wrong. What was truly wrong. She would be understanding and talk me through it. She would be a friend - maybe offer some advice. She would be there for me.

Those all seemed like good options. False hope is still hope - my therapist would say. I stepped back into the kitchen and Trish was picking up the tea. She grabbed a bag of English Breakfast, opened it, and poured the hot water. As she met my gaze I mouthed, "I'm sorry."

I started on my coffee and gave an audible sigh. Here goes nothing. "My husband cheated. Before he died, obviously, whatever. Anyway, he had an affair with someone we went to school with. Her name was Audrey. She could not be more opposite of me. He said it only happened for a few weeks, but I won't ever really know. I caught him so he didn't confess. When you catch people lying it's worse - you know. It makes them a coward and a liar."

Trish sat and steeped her tea. She gave me a nod to continue.

"Well, he had a car accident shortly after that. When he died, part of me was relieved we wouldn't have to work through it. Part of me was hysterical over having lost the love of my life. He WAS the love of my life. His infidelity didn't change that I loved him. We had a baby and I was alone. It was awful. I haven't dated anyone since."

"Until Milo," Trish finally spoke.

"That's right. He got caught too. Lying about who he was."

There was a long pause before Trish said anything. She had to think about what to say, and I respected that. When she finally spoke, she put her palms flat on the table and looked up into my eyes.

"I'm so sorry about what you went through. I cannot imagine the strength it took you to survive that."

My tears threatened to escape again. I sniffled and puffed my chest looking up at the kitchen lights to gain control. "Thank you," I whispered.

Trish stood and had me in a hug. "You are amazing, Mel. I'm so glad I'm getting to know you better."

"I just felt like Milo could be the person. For some reason, I'm here. And now it's all gone to shit," I sniffled.

"Are you so sure he's not? I know that's not what you want to hear and feel free to slap me right across the face for saying it, but I've known Milo my whole life. He hasn't had a serious girlfriend in the last decade. You come to town and he's living here again. He's all about you. The last time I've heard him upset is when he put his father in a home. He seemed worse this morning."

My heart fluttered a bit at her account of Milo's love life. He said he had been writing to me for ten years. Was that why he had the dry spell?

"What happened with him and Paul?" I asked.

Trish raised her eyebrows and lifted her hands to her hips. "You mean Marshall?" she said. "No one has called him Paul since primary school." She gave me a sideways glance but didn't question my intimate knowledge about his name.

"Okay where to start? So, Marshall and Milo were awfully close among the four, which made their mum upset at times. Milo has a different biological mother." She lowered her voice, "An affair."

I nodded and made a motion with my hand for her to continue.

"When Marshall went to university, he met Claudia. She was bloody awful. I won't get into everything, but it about tore the brothers apart. In the end, Claudia had laundered some money from the brothers' business. Some isn't right... She started doing their accounting and about cleaned them out. Marshall took his wife's side and things weren't the same after that. They all moved away from each other, and we didn't see them together much anymore. I'm sure there is a lot more, but Claudia should have been in jail is how I understood it. Looking back, she was isolating Marshall. If she hadn't been caught with the money, he and his brothers may not have any relationship at all. It planted a seed of doubt in Marshall. The brothers keep in touch still, so that's something."

"At least I think Marshall and Claudia are still married," she continued.

"Oh, they are," I shot back.

Trish threw her hands in the air. "Bloody hell, Mel. What is going on?"

"How many life events do you have time for?" I said.

"All of them. Milo would not tell me details."

I spent the next hour going over the high points of the night. Trish seemed more interested in hearing about the sex than the massive confession of betrayal. I had glazed over the importance of my relationship with Paul. It sounded tragic when I said it out loud. Like I wanted him all my life. *Did I?*

After time with Trish - a text from Rita that she was fine to have the kids - and some bourbon in my coffee, I felt better. Trish made me go through my texts and voicemails while she was with me - just in case I had a complete meltdown. It was much of what

I expected until I got to the last voicemail from the unknown number.

Mel this is Paul. I know you may not want to see me, but I am desperate to see you. I'll be at the Hamblin coffee shop after work every day this week for a few hours. Please come talk to me. I'm sorry. I hope you come. I...I...um well, Mel, you know I care. I just .... a lot happened and it won't fit on your voicemail. Please come to see me. You can come in just to hit me if you want. Please, Mel.

Trish's jaw hung open. She started to collect her things in silence. She had an opinion I could tell.

"What is it, Trish?" I said.

She lowered her shoulders and pursed her lips. "I just think you HAVE to see him, and I'm worried you will skip out. Get Rita to go with you and sit in the corner. Mrs. MacArthur will watch the children. She's familiar with the happenings around here. She probably already knows all about the brother switch up."

"I'll think about it," I promised her. "Thank you for listening to my rants this morning. Tomorrow let's run please. I'll need it."

When she left the house, I started to stress clean. Picking up leftover wine glasses and making the bed, I wanted to erase any memory of the night before. My new lingerie lay on the floor in a pile and I threw it in the hamper in the corner. A lot of good they did me.

Milo's shirt was the last thing left on my bedroom floor. I picked it up and felt the fabric in my fingers. It smelled like him, a mix of mint and woods. I couldn't talk to him. I wanted him still, but I hated him more. I threw the shirt with the other clothes and stormed into the living room. Before I could give it a second thought, I texted Paul.

I'll see you Monday

CHAPTER 25

I dressed like I was preparing for battle Monday morning - straight leg black pants and sky-high heels paired with a royal blue long sleeve wrap shirt. I wore Chanel earrings Rita had gifted me and put my hair in a high slick pony. I was rocking the sex and power look, but it was only six in the morning.

I called the company car to get me early. It was available for early and late workdays and I wanted to take off Wednesday for the kids' first day of school. I also wanted to avoid Milo and working four ten-hour days was a good way around it.

I made it to the office before seven and got loads accomplished before Rita strolled in around nine.

"Trish and I had drinks last night," she hollered through the open conference room doors. That had been by design. On our Sunday run, I asked Trish to get with Rita and fill her in. I didn't have the physical energy to tell the story again. It was a risk that she would get pissed hearing it from Trish, but I crossed my fingers she would forgive me.

It was first come first served right now with me. Apparently with men and friends. I hissed at myself at the thought.

"Are you very angry I didn't tell you myself?" I shouted back.

I could hear her hanging her coat and setting down her things. She stepped in my doorway a few moments later, crossed her arms, and shifted to one hip. "I've been too enthralled with Robert's dick, I get it. I've abandoned my friend duties. Chicks before dicks from now on."

Her cool smile told me she wasn't holding any grudges. "You are here early," she continued. "Milo wasn't on the bus this morning. He won't be I'm guessing."

"You're right," I said. "But why not use the company car while I can. I've submitted our initial projections four days ahead of schedule, so they won't say anything about it."

"And I'm guessing we will use it on our way home after your, um, date. Not a date I suppose. Your inquisition rather?" Rita raised her eyebrows.

"You don't have to come. I don't think we should leave the kids with Mrs. MacArthur that long,"

"Bollocks. She told me she is going to fall into depression when they start school this week and asked to keep them later."

I looked up at her and started laughing. "Bollocks? You are spending too much time with Robert."

"Disagree, but I'll refrain from the British slang. Unless you are enjoying it, and right now you could use a laugh."

"I'm nervous enough without an audience. I appreciate your

support, but I need to do this on my own."

Rita walked in and sat in one of the chairs in front of my desk. She had a tight smile as she crossed her legs and arms. "I know you can do this and I know you are strong. Stronger than most of us."

I closed my laptop and squinted at her. "What's going on?" I said. "You seem a bit on edge. I am sorry that Trish has been there for more of the, um, life events. Milo events, I guess. It's not intentional. I love you. You know that."

"And I love you very much," Rita murmured. "So, let's remember that when I tell you something."

I gave my chair a scoot forward and my heart started to beat faster. "Tell me what Rita?"

"Okay I'm just going to speed through this, so if at all possible, try to hide your reaction so I don't chicken out."

"What is it, Rita?" I grumbled.

Rita shifted side to side in her chair. This woman could fake comfort if she were caught on fire. This wasn't going to be good.

"I emailed Paul last week," she revealed. "Specifically, I emailed him before you agreed to search Milo and Paul. Anyway, once you had greenlit the investigation, I used his reply and searched his IP address. I took the pilot Prometheus code to determine the exact location. Tad bit illegal it turns out according to our incredibly nervous twenty-five-year-old IT coconspirator, so if we could keep that between us gals, I would be super appreciative."

"What did you email him?" I demanded.

"Not really important in this confession, but okay, um, basically why are you such a pussy?"

I dropped my head in my hands. "Seriously Rita?"

"Well, he wrote you a Dear Jane letter after all these years. Total puss."

I stared at her wide-eyed. "I told you specifically not to do that. What did he respond?"

"Some bullshit, which now makes more sense considering your current situation."

I huffed at her and made a choking motion with my hands to her neck.

"See that's not hiding your reaction," Rita continued. "Anyway, his email back, now that I reread it, was asking a lot of questions about the letter. It was veiled, I don't think that he knew what he wrote. I mean...that is, if he wrote it. I think you got an authentic Paul letter in the mix. This whole thing is kind of fucked up."

She made a jack-off motion with her hand, but I didn't laugh.

"Okay so the meat and potatoes of this is that the location was Winlin Ave," she blurted out, crossing her arms tighter around her body.

I squinted at her and cocked my head. I tried to compute what she was telling me, but I couldn't put the puzzle pieces together.

Rita took a big breath and carried on, "At the time, I thought Milo was Paul. I genuinely believed that night he was going to confess who he was and that he was leaving his wife. In fairness, the latter part could still be happening."

I sat back and took in all the information. I understood Rita's conclusions. Everything had happened quickly, and she was laser-focused on Paul and me getting together whatever the cost. She couldn't have known what was coming based on what she knew at the time. Hell, no one saw this coming.

"Now is the time to react because you look kind of dumbfounded," she begged.

"You should have told me about the location," I snapped.

"Yes, I should have and I'm sorry."

"And you should not have tried to dress me up like a sex kitten to try and get Paul to leave his wife."

"Agree to disagree," she said giving me a sideways smile. "Okay, I'm sorry about that. But you did get it good that night from what I hear."

"And you aren't coming tonight," I insisted.

She bit her lip and looked down at her knees. "How about I go to the restaurant next door. I could stay in the area, but not invade on your conversation."

"That's a nice offer, but again no. I need to do this on my own. I've had a lot of people make decisions on my behalf lately which left me in this mess."

Rita's eyes started to well up. That one cut deep, and I didn't want to hurt her. I reached out and put my hand palm up on the desk. She reached out and held it.

"Are we okay?" she choked out.

"Is anyone ever okay? But this isn't something I'm going to dwell on anymore. So, two promises now. Stay with me when we go out and no more trickery for my own good."

Rita squeezed my hand. "Trish said that night at the club worked out for you too," she smirked.

I flushed immediately. As confused and frustrated as I was about Milo, thinking of him still gave me goosebumps. *Stop it, Mel.*

Rita rose and lifted her finger. "I have a gift for you," she said rushing out of my office. When she came back in, she was holding another manilla folder. "I didn't read this one. I was told it doesn't hold a lot of dirt, but who knows. Yours to peruse dear."

I took the folder. "Is this on Paul or Milo?"

"I don't know because I DIDN'T READ THIS ONE," She bellowed. "Just delivered this on my desk this morning. I'm going to have to motorboat this guy for all this research. Or maybe get him a nice hooker. Like a cute one."

We both snickered. She walked around my desk and hugged me, and we got back to work. We were both still ahead. So ahead in fact, that I wasn't worried Rita had used the program for our personal needs - something that in the past would throw me in a complete panic. We were rock stars on this deal. Maybe I was a disaster on the love end of things, but I wouldn't fail here.

Five o'clock came and went, but Paul could wait. Rita came by my office with Lynn asking again if I was sure I wanted to go by myself. I knew they would talk about my state of affairs the entire way home, but I didn't care. They can make a Mel-drama-phone-tree. I'll just have to confide in one of them and, poof, all are up

139

to date. After convincing her I would be fine, she conceded.

After another thirty minutes of stalling, checking my makeup, and giving myself the happy outcome pep talk I had used way too many times since moving here, I left the office. When I hit the elevator button my nerves bubbled in my stomach.

I had no plan for what I was walking into and I hadn't opened the file Rita had given me yet. The wing-it approach seemed to be my thing so far. The jury was out on if it was working well or not. What are you going to ask him? Don't ramble, let him dig his own grave.

When I walked up to The Hamblin Café, I could feel my pulse in my whole body. Paul was sitting in a corner booth with a cup in front of him. He had on a white dress shirt with the top two buttons undone. I considered walking up to the table and throwing his drink on him and grinned to myself. I stood close to the brick wall by the window where he couldn't see me.

He was handsome like Milo. I imagined all the brothers had that quality. They both had broad shoulders and sharp jawlines. His face was softer somehow, maybe features from his mother. His eyes a bit larger and his cheekbones are less defined.

He was worried. He had waited for over an hour already. His brow was furrowed, and he kept tapping on the table with some paper in his hands. I felt a pang of guilt about that now. I'm sure this wasn't easy for him, or any of us. I had made it harder on purpose.

I exhaled and turned away from the window. Leaning against the brick wall I closed my eyes and focused on calming myself. I had to do this. I had to talk to him. Whatever the history was, not knowing was worse.

Deep breaths, Mel.

I opened my eyes feeling no more ready to face him but resigned to it. I needed to know exactly how much of my past was a complete lie. A husband who cheated and a friend that deceived me. It would hurt, hell it already did, but I could survive anything at this point.

What I saw stopped me in my tracks.

A man standing across the street in agony. Sunken eyes and sullen expression. The way he looked at me sent a sharp pain to my chest. His eyes bore into mine with desperation. He just stared. Neither of us moved as my eyes pricked with tears.

I wanted him.

He lit me on fire.

Milo

CHAPTER 26

I reached back for the wall behind me and led myself towards the front door of the café. We didn't break our gaze. I couldn't. He had me in a spell where it physically hurt to look away from him.

I hated how broken he was. Like a man who had been beaten and thrown out to the garbage. Still handsome without trying, but his face was twisted in anguish. I held the handle of the front door and yanked it open. Before I turned, I saw him mouth I love you, and I threw myself into the café, tears falling steadily now.

Not how I wanted to greet Paul. Totally off the boss bitch vibe I was shooting for.

Paul must have seen me walking past the windows. He was at my side and gently clutched my elbow and led me to the table. He was quiet for a moment but broke the silence with something about not being happy to see him. His voice was muddled and I had to compose myself before speaking.

"Milo's out there," I sputtered. My eyes had dried up and I caught the waitress. I had enough self-control to order tea and a muffin.

"Is he coming in?" Paul asked.

"He won't," I answered.

Paul raised one eyebrow and handed me a napkin. "Milo hasn't been the best at controlling himself lately."

"He won't," I snapped. I took my phone out and switched my camera to my face. Nothing was abhorrent about my appearance. I dabbed under my eyes and moved my focus to Paul. "You should start talking."

Paul's back straightened. He looked me over and flashed a small smile. "You look more beautiful than I could have imagined," he choked out.

"I don't think Claudia would appreciate that comment," I said unsmiling.

"Claudia and I have separated." He folded his hands together and glared down at them. "That doesn't matter, but I wanted you to know. I'm not a cheater."

"Not like my husband," I said.

"Your late husband, and no."

A moment of silence swept over us as the server brought over my tea. His comment was honest but infuriating. I had confided Mitch's infidelities to Paul. Although at that time I guess Milo was the one getting them. We hadn't been sending many letters back and forth at that point, but getting several letters in the span of a month from me about my husband cheating and then becoming comatose because of a drunk driver jumpstarted our communication.

I steeped my tea and swallowed hard. "I need you to start somewhere. Really anywhere will do right now Paul. Or is it Marshall?"

"It's always Paul with you Mel," he said reaching a hand towards mine. I jerked back and almost spilled my tea. He continued, "I went by Paul in primary school for a short while when we started writing. It was Maxwell, Marcus, and Marshall. Three brothers almost Irish triplets back to back. Mum dressed us alike and we had our own language. Hell, we would walk in step down the street. I wanted to be different, so I started to go by my middle name. When Milo came around, we clicked instantly. I wanted to be back alike with them again - with him - so I started to go by Marshall and called it a phase."

"I know Milo has a different mother," I said.

"Yes, he does," Paul sighed. "Milo and I are only a few months apart if that tells you anything. His mother committed suicide and he came to live with us as boys. My mum loved and hated him all the same. You need to know how close we were to understand. How close we are. I hope we still are." He took a sip of his tea and I fought the urge to reach my hand to his. He was hurting, but it was still his doing.

"Is that why you all played this joke together?" I uttered fidgeting with my cup.

"No," he almost shouted. "I mean no there is no joke. We didn't do that." He ran his hand through his hair roughly and bit his bottom lip. "That wasn't what happened."

"Well what did happen?" I clipped.

He took a ragged breath and reached for my hand again. I didn't pull away this time, and I didn't know why. He held it rubbing his thumb gently back and forth over my skin.

"Claudia and I had problems in the beginning. You should know that you weren't a contributor, but there was a time where she made me feel like you were. She wanted me to stop writing to you and we fought about it often. I tried to space out letters to perhaps stop them, but I just kept thinking about what you were doing or how you were. I would have something I just felt I had to tell you and then, it just...."

"You missed me," I said.

His eyes met mine. "Yes, I did very much."

"I confided in Milo when Claudia and I were at our breaking point. I was very torn. I didn't know why at the time. Milo offered to take over the letters and cut it off. We moved them to a post office box, and he would give me an overview of what you wrote or what he wrote. I ... I couldn't end it. But maybe he could."

He kept holding my hand and cleared his throat. "When Mitch died," he paused. This part was hard for us both. I could tell he was pulling away all those years ago. I thought it was our age and distance and time. I know now, it was actually Milo pulling away.

"When he did what he did to you," he continued. "And then when you had to do what you did. When he died Mel, Milo just couldn't let you go. He didn't tell me at first. Not everything. Later he said he thought I would be upset, and then he grew defiant. Claudia and I moved further away from town, and he had cut me off from the communication between you both for a time. I knew it was still happening. I didn't fight him hard enough on it.

Even though it was him writing to you, it still meant you were in my life."

He squeezed my hand harder. "After a few years, I asked to read the letters. We fought, and I said things I shouldn't have. I'm ashamed of what I said to him, Mel. I agreed to keep his identity a secret, and he agreed to leave the letters out when I would visit. I would read a years' worth of life in a day. It broke my heart," he trailed off.

I could feel my body inhale unsteady breaths. I knew what I wanted to ask. It came out so soft he could barely hear me. I had to repeat myself.

"Why were you torn. Between me and Claudia," I almost whispered.

Paul raised my hand to his cheek. He was burning up. The way he looked at me made heat rush over my skin. He clutched me as if I would run at his answer.

"I love you, Mel," he said. "I wanted you. I .... I have a lot of regrets."

I tried to pull my hand back, but it wouldn't budge. *Is that what I wanted to hear?*

"Paul," I said. "You feel that way because you are going through a separation. When was the last time you wrote me a letter? You, yourself, and not Milo."

"I wrote one about Claudia not knowing about you," he said. "I didn't tell Milo about it. That's the most recent, but there are many more."

With that, he pulled the pages he had been holding earlier from the seat next to him along with a small leather notebook. "These," he said. "I didn't mail them, any of them. I'll never forgive myself for that. I want you to have them now. This book too."

I took the small leather notebook in my hands. The spine was soft and creased from use.

"Do you remember that?" Paul asked.

I did. It was the book I sent him when his mother died. I opened it and flipped through the pages. Every page was filled top to bottom. A few dates I saw went back to the year she passed away.

I nodded slightly and closed the book. "You want me to have this?"

"You said it wasn't a diary, and it wasn't. It turned into more of a confessional. You can read it, but I would like it back. It's one of the few things that brings me joy anymore. Writing about you when I couldn't write to you."

CHAPTER 27

Dear Mel,

11th November 2010

I'm going to start this letter Mission Impossible-style. It's one you should light on fire once read because I'm not smart enough to make it self-combust.

You may not want to keep this, and you may hate me for writing this. If that's the case, throw it in the fire and we won't speak of it again. I can play along like it never happened.

Claudia and I are in the weeds of planning this wedding. Every night is seating plans and tastings. She obsesses over the registry and worries if she will get all the Waterford Crystal she cannot live without. The wedding planner seems completely overwhelmed with her demands and I'm tipping her weekly - so she doesn't run.

I couldn't care less.

Are you happier in your planning? Do you wish we could attend each other's events? You being on your honeymoon during our nuptials it would never have worked, but would you want to join?

I wouldn't go to your wedding.

I think we are both making a mistake.

I don't think I want to marry Claudia anymore and I think you feel the same way about Mitch. When something great happens, it's you I want to tell. When something terrible happens, it's you. I haven't called or set up a visit because I'm a coward. If I held you, it would be over for me. You would be the one and I was scared.

My sensible side wouldn't allow it. You live on the other side of the world and the fact that I ended up in this mess - engaged - is beyond me. How did it get this far for either of us?

We should be together.

Mitch does not love you as I do. He won't love you in the future the way I will. I know everything about you and I'm obsessed with all of it. You're like a limb to me. There is a piece of me missing without you.

To him, you are an accessory. He loves himself more, and I would never do that.

I can book either of us a flight if you say yes.

Love,

Paul

P.S. Ring me so we don't waste any more time.

CHAPTER 28

That letter was the summation of all the others. Each had small confessions of feelings or even love, but the request to call off our weddings left me in shambles. Paul said he wanted me to read them all before we kept talking. He left the café as I started shuffling through the pages.

I could barely make it through the first year of his notebook. I skimmed until I got to fall, 2009. I knew what I would read but I wanted to feel it - how hurt he was for what I had done. I needed to know that it wasn't just me who was depressed over my choice of Mitch over Paul. That's what I had done. I had made a choice, and I had chosen the easy way out.

December 4th, 2009. Mel wrote another letter asking if I was angry with her. Fuck yes - I'm angry with her. I haven't told her because I don't want to hurt her. Claudia is sleeping next to me right now and I wish it was Mel. She could have come up this summer and we could have tried. She could be in my bed. I dream about being inside her. Mitch will throw her away like rubbish. I would have cherished her. I would have ruined her. She chose a boring life in a boring town with boring sex. I would have made it so she couldn't stand going back to that. She would never settle for any other man if I had her, and now I'm supposed to write to her that everything is fine while I'm fucking Claudia and thinking about Mel.

The company car came to get me and I closed the book. I couldn't string two words together with the driver. I didn't notice if Milo was still outside or not. I could have walked out without pants on and not noticed. Shock was an understatement. I didn't have words for my feelings.

I thought back on my engagement with Mitch. I was obsessed with the thought of being married and having children. Every other weekend there was a wedding or engagement or gender reveal or some other major life event. I had never thought myself a follower, but when that train started, there was no stopping.

I wanted in.

There was a moment during the planning that reminded me of Paul's letter. We had to increase the catering again because Mitch had invited more work acquaintances. Wanting to impress the boss, they all would come. He was a rising star at his company, and I thought he was using our day to show off. We fought and I called the wedding a circus.

In my gut though I felt it was too late. I remembered thinking I'm stuck, the invites are sent, can't go back now.

On the day of my wedding, my maid of honor sat me down and gave me the official out. She said if I wanted to run to Mexico, she would take care of everything. I acted like she was insane. She said she gave that offer to anyone getting married just in case, but I don't think she did.

The week prior I had discovered Mitch made out with a woman at his bachelor party. I brushed it off as a last crazy night, but I knew. I never confronted him about it.

I knew then. *You're such a coward Mel.*

I loved Mitch, but I romanticized us. I went through the motions and played the game to fit in. Wedding and baby and parties and bullshit.

It was all bullshit.

Paul committed the same sin. How many of us do that?

When I arrived home, the whole gang of women greeted me, each holding a bottle of wine. Rita double fisting with vodka. I liked options.

"You bitches are amazing," I said. Rita, Trish, and Lynn gave me hugs and a huge glass. I could hear Eva and Jack playing in the bedroom and promised them one more hour until we started bedtime. They replied in unison, "Okay." We had to get them a routine or school would be disastrous.

I handed Rita the letters and plopped down in my corner chair – keeping the notebook to myself. The ladies crowded behind her as she read. I watched their eyes widen and jaws drop as I sipped (chugged) my drink.

"Well, let me have it," I said. Rita had been waiting for this moment. I drank the glass ready for the firing range.

Rita slapped her hands on her thighs, "I literally have no words. I mean, I wanted there to be a romance there, but wow. I kind of figured there would be something like this though. And he's married to this awful woman but in love with you."

Lynn and Trish nodded in unison reaching for another bottle.

"He's separated from Claudia."

Trish spit out her drink.

"Oh my God," Trish said wiping her chin. "I thought that would never happen. Did he leave her for you?"

"No," I snapped. "At least I don't think so. We didn't get into the specifics, he just said they were separated. And Milo was at the café. I mean not in the café, but he was across the street and he looked completely depressed. I just wanted to run up and kiss him. But then I was sitting there with Paul and I had this vision of what our life could be or what it would have been. And I'm pissed because he should have just sent the damn letter. And Paul was getting Milo to be his shadow writer to break up with me. Break off the friendship I mean because he couldn't."

"Because he loves you," Rita interjected.

"Apparently," I continued. "So, for ten years, I repeat, TEN YEARS LADIES, Milo has been his Cyrano. Milo never once wrote a letter with feelings either. It isn't until I get here and he's all creepy sexy stalker that I think this must be fate because he feels so familiar. But no, it turns out he just knows every intimate detail of my life playing Paul. What is that? I mean what the actual fuck is that? And why is my luggage over there?"

"Oh," Lynn said. "Because we are taking you away this weekend —

to Cornwall."

"What!" I shrieked spilling my wine.

"Yes, so Friday you and Rita are leaving at lunch and we are going on a girl's trip. You need it. We all need it really and you are a convenient excuse."

"Robert has a house there," Rita chimed in. "We can stay for free and Mrs. MacArthur has agreed to have the kids for the weekend. She's already sad about not having them all day anymore. Please don't argue because I repeat, we need to get away."

"I have nothing to add, but I was told there would be unlimited alcohol," Trish said raising her glass. "I dislike most females, but you birds seem alright."

I almost doubled over laughing. The whole situation was completely preposterous. There was a man I knew my whole life, but I didn't know him at all, a man I barely knew, but who knew everything about me and knew me intimately. And these ladies, who sat on my sofa smiling and drinking, eager for me to say yes to a spontaneous getaway.

A month ago, I would have thought this entire day would be impossible. My life was a string of days I never thought would happen. I suppose everyone's life comes down to that.

"Why the hell not," I said raising my glass. "Maybe when we get back, I'll know what I'm doing."

"Or who you are doing," Lynn smirked.

CHAPTER 29

Wednesday came and went without a hitch. I made everyone a huge breakfast which the kids barely touched, but whatever. Flowers and candy were delivered to the house from Mrs. MacArthur because she's amazing and knew exactly what would make the kid's first day of school perfect.

Rita was there for breakfast and drop-off but had to leave right after. I promised to come back for lunch and Eva and Jack were unimpressed. Eva informed me I would be embarrassing, and I lost Jack's interest as soon as we hit the school grounds.

I took it all as a good sign that they were happy with their new school and not clinging to my legs like babies. It stung a little, but this was the best outcome for everyone. The school was walking distance, so I gave them lunch money, and taking the hint they wanted me gone fast I started back to the house. I passed by Mrs. MacArthur's on the way and dropped in to thank her for the goodies.

She was on the porch as I walked up. "Having some tea?" I asked taking a seat in the rocker next to her.

"Mel, dear how are you. I'm just a wreck without those lambs," she answered. "Did you get my delivery this morning?"

"I did and I'm here to thank you, and to chat as well. You take such good care of us. We don't deserve you."

She smiled and waved her hand in the air. "Darling, I love those kids and you. I'm grateful."

"I took the day off thinking the kids may - I don't know - call me to get them or something. They seem to just want me gone - so now I have the day to myself."

"Maybe some time for reflection dear," she said as she took a sip. She rocked quietly and looked me over. Of course, she knew about Paul and Milo. She likely knew all along, but it wasn't her place to tell. It also takes Rita a solid hour to get home with the kids because she's here gossiping, so my privacy doesn't stand a chance.

"So, what have you heard lately?" I asked. A large thud from inside her house made me jump. "What was that?"

She stopped rocking and looked back at her front door. "Oh, never mind that dear," she waved off the noise. "But I've heard enough to warn you Milo is working on a burst pipe in the living area." I froze immediately and she gave me a wink.

"Does he know I'm here?" I whispered.

"Your guess is as good as mine," she replied. "Maybe he saw you coming up the steps and plans to flood the place in a jealous rage. Young love. So full of passion and stupidity. God, I miss it."

"Have you seen the movie Freaky Friday, Mrs. MacArthur?"

"I don't miss it that much, dear. You need to sort this love triangle out on your own."

I rocked and pursed my lips at her while she sipped. The curtains were pulled back, but I couldn't see Milo. Maybe he saw me, chucked his wrench, and ran out the back. *You're the runner, Mel, not him.*

Mrs. MacArthur resumed her rocking and patted me on the shoulder. "I could use a refill on my tea Carmela," she said with a sly look. "It would be good for both of us."

"Sure thing," I said gritting my teeth. "I heard the Wag has the best breakfast tea and I'd love to see Trish. Let's go."

Mrs. MacArthur's face fell. "Get in the house, Mel. Trust me when I say you are further in your story than you realize."

With that, I rose with a deep inhale. I needed the push but immediately regretted my morning attire. I was wearing black leggings and a T-Shirt from a charity event back in Maine. My hair was in a messy pony and I didn't have on any makeup. *Oh shit, maybe Eva was right about me embarrassing her.*

I ran my hands down the front of my shirt and made a face. "Your arse is still above your knees and bras are optional for you darling, so I wouldn't worry about it," Mrs. MacArthur quipped. We both let out a loud cackle and I heard boots coming towards the porch. She shoved her cup in my hands and I shuffled towards the front door with a pout.

When I entered the house, Milo was only a few feet away. He had a sheen of sweat on his chest and a tool in one hand. He swallowed hard when he saw me and I watched his Adams Apple rise and fall. I walked past him with my head down and made my way to the kitchen.

As I started the kettle, the clang of the tool hit the counter. "Careful," I murmured. "You wouldn't want that to scratch."

"It's my counter," he said. "I own this home as well." He shook his head and cracked his knuckles. "But yes, I would never want to damage anything in Mrs. MacArthur's house. She wants the Earl Grey."

I had been sifting through the basket of tea at her table aimlessly. "Thank you," I barely got out. I grabbed the tray of milk and sugar and headed towards the door. He was in step behind me but said nothing. With my hands full, he reached around my body and opened the front door.

I slid out and set the tray down. "Anything else I can get for you?" I asked Mrs. MacArthur.

"No dear," she beamed eyes darting between us both.

"We are taking a walk," Milo growled taking my arm and leading me down the front steps. I shot a look for help thinking I may be sick, but Mrs. MacArthur was giving me no out whatsoever. "How nice dears. Take your time."

His grip wasn't soft or kind, but I had missed his touch. Heat spread all through my body and my breathing became erratic. His effect on me was immediate and intense.

We were almost jogging back to the house. "I'm ready to talk about this with you," I croaked. *He's not giving me a choice, but I can at least act like it's my idea.*

"Paul said you were supposed to end the letters, but you didn't.

He used the word defiant. Why did you keep this up? Why wouldn't you just tell me who you were? Why are we running?"

Milo said nothing but his grip on my arm tightened. Something I said struck a nerve. We rushed up the stairs and through my front door. When it slammed behind him, he whipped me around so we were face to face. Both his hands clutched the sides of my arms and held me in place.

I was terrified and relieved to be in front of him. He knew me so well and I could tell he wanted me. Every sharp edge of his face made my sex clench. Every muscle on his torso begged for me to touch him.

"I told you I would answer any questions you have, and I meant that," he snarled. He was angry hearing me speak Paul's name. I realized that now. Bringing up our conversation at the café ripped him apart.

He continued, "I told him I would end the letters, but I couldn't. You were funny and charming and empathic and I wanted to know everything about you - the way you thought about things, your outlook on life, your sense of humor. I wish you could see yourself the way others do, the way I do. You would be amazed. You would be in love."

His words cut through me and I started to tear up. He knew all the dark parts – all the terrible choices – and loved me.

"I cannot put into words how hard it was to defy my brother, to risk our bond, to keep in contact with you," he persisted. "But I won't ever regret that. I also can't explain how it was for me being rejected every damn day by my own family. You know I had a different mother, but you can't imagine hating who you are."

He started to shake in rage and was now gently shaking me as he spat out the words, "I was an outcast every single day Mel. There were days Paul's mother couldn't look at me without crying. There were days they forgot me going to church. I sat at a different table at dinner because there wasn't room. I spent a lifetime in a home reminded hourly that my brothers were preferred. My brothers were wanted and I was not. How did I think it would be if you had to choose between me and Paul? It's tattooed on my brain that he's better."

He glimpsed at the wall next to us with the gaping hole. He released my arms slightly and stepped forward. We were almost touching. I was trembling at his confessions. This strong and seemingly confident man in front of me who was once an excluded little boy. My heart bled for the shattered spirit of that child.

"How do I fare now, Mel? Now that you know."

His hands lifted to my face tilting my chin upwards. He crashed his mouth to mine and I opened in response. I moaned at the feel of his tongue and melted into him wrapping my arms around his back.

In a swift movement, he lifted me into his arms and started towards the bedroom. He threw me on the bed and started removing his clothes. "Do you want to talk?" he drawled, lowering his jeans. I shook my head defiantly - NO - as I ripped my shirt off from over my head. Hooking his hands over the tops of my leggings he pulled them off in one motion as I yanked my sports bra over my head. *Not exactly the couture lingerie today so best to just rip it off.*

He lowered on top of me, both of us naked and panting. "I don't want to talk either love. Part of me can't know yet," he growled. I could see the veins in his neck throbbing. I could feel his length hard against my stomach. "But right now, you are mine. In my bed and in my arms. It will be my dick inside you. Do you understand?"

I nodded and gasped, "Yes."

"And you need to be mine right now, don't you?" he persisted.

"Yes," I answered. "I've always needed you."

He started down my body kissing my neck, sucking my nipples. Making his way to my stomach he yanked my body to the edge of the bed and hung my knees over his shoulders. I cried out when his hot mouth fell on my flesh and my whimpers continued as he worked me with his tongue. My hands ran through his hair pushing him into me as I flexed my hips in rhythm. He groaned into my body at my response to him.

When I reached climax all my worries and fears went blank. Life felt perfect in my waves of pleasure. When I climaxed three more times over the next two hours, I couldn't even spell the word worry if my life depended on it.

Milo was unyielding in his control, tossing me around the bed like a rag doll. When he relented and his caress became gentle, I was sure he was checking me for bruises.

"I'm fine," I whispered curling up next to him.

Milo rubbed his palm up my back and pulled me into his chest. "I was too rough. I'm sorry." He set his chin on top of my head.

"You weren't," I insisted. "Telling me about your childhood was difficult and I understand you had some misplaced …. anger maybe? You know like you had to …. I don't know."

"Fuck it out of my system?" he laughed.

"Maybe?" I giggled in response. "But no matter what happens, I'm sorry you went through that. I'm sorry you feel less than."

He stilled his breathing and started to speak, but then bit his lip. He wanted to ask me if he was less than Paul. He wasn't, but that didn't mean I was sure about my feelings for him or Paul.

I interrupted before he could get the words out. "I'm going away this weekend with the girls, and I'll be with the kids and Rita this week out of – you know – mom guilt. I'm not going to waste too much time figuring this out okay. We have …. chemistry, that's for sure. But you did the one thing that I can't easily forgive."

"I deceived you," he sighed.

"Yes, and if you – and Paul – could lie for years about this, you could lie about, anything really."

"I would never cheat on you, Mel. I didn't go and get married to some bitch because you lived too far away."

I quieted at his response. There was no way he was celibate for ten years, not with the way he knew how to make love to a woman, but he wasn't married. Solid points for that. I sat up and started to dress and he followed suit.

I checked my phone and saw only messages from Rita with pictures from this morning. "I'll call you when I'm back I promise. I'm not about wasting time. Not anymore"

Milo stared at his phone in contempt.

"What is it?" I asked.

Milo shoved the phone in his pocket and reached for his shirt. Something had set him off. He stomped toward the front door.

"Hey," I shouted. He spun himself around. "What's with the bi-polar shit? Not a great way to leave me you know."

His face softened as he came back to me, placing a gentle kiss on my lips.

"Love, I heard you and I hope you have a good trip. I – I just …. Paul messaged me. He wants to get together."

"And you should. You have to talk to him."

"I may not get the choice," Milo clipped, running his hand through his hair. I squinted with a muddled expression.

Milo exhaled heavily. "He lives here now - in Winlin. He separated from Claudia. And he knows I'm here – with you. He knows I'm here right now."

CHAPTER 30

Milo left with my mouth still gaping open. Paul came here for me, there was no other explanation. I had visions of a wild west standoff between brothers. Tumbleweeds and pistols.

Nope!

Friday afternoon took forever to arrive. No sightings of Paul, but I avoided the bar, going for a run, going outside unless necessary, and opening my curtains. Solid plan which was working splendidly. He had messaged me to meet again without giving away his location. Did he know Milo told me? I only responded to him once saying I was going away for the weekend and I wasn't ready to talk until I came back.

I could not trust myself alone with Milo and I wasn't ready to test the waters with Paul and take permanent residence in Slutsville. *Oh God, what if they were alike.*

Rita walked into my office while I was shaking my head at the thought murmuring, "no - no – no."

"Yes – Yes – Yes!" she said. "It's time – let's scoot. I'm SO excited. We already have reservations for dinner on a yacht that specializes in wine flights."

"I heard wine," Lynn bellowed from the hallway. I could see heads turn at the desks out front. Lord these women did NOT give two shits what people thought. I loved it.

She took out a bottle from her bag and made a smack with her lips on the label. "Why are you not ready? Our car leaves in just enough time for us to pick up Trish and down this bottle – and then like two more. Maybe three."

Rita started rolling her carry-on through the hall and I scrambled to catch up to them. I wasn't sure if this trip was for me or my clan of females, but I could not wipe the smile off my face.

We had successfully emptied a few bottles and reached a pleasant shade of tipsy when we boarded the yacht. Rita had used an intern to run around the city chasing weekend getaway looks with her credit card. Not a bad gig and we all benefited from new outfits.

I had on white linen pants, a matching halter top, and tan Tory Burch sandals. Lynn and Rita donned maxi dresses with an obnoxious amount of side boob, and Trish had a jumper that showed off her curves in the best ways.

We were winning the yacht life, but does anyone ever lose boarding a beautiful boat with friends, wine, and food? We sat in a large round booth facing the water. A cool breeze floated through us as gourmet food was dropped tray after tray at our table. Wine samplings came soon after with an excited sommelier spouting off loads of facts and figures about our options.

As an equal opportunity wine lover, everything sounded great.

I'm sure there is something to be said for organic, barrel-aged, small-batch, young vines, and blah bitty blah, but just give me fermented grapes, please.

"Cheers mate," Trish gave his palm a light tap, politely telling him exit. He scurried away, still murmuring something about wine crystals. "So, Rita. We are staying at Roberts posh villa. Are you taking him up on his offer then?"

I looked around trying to gauge the group's reaction. Rita reddened and started in on some hors d'oeuvres. Robert's home was unbelievable. Only hours before, Trish was walking around the perfectly decorated rooms, two kitchens, and a full-size pool saying "This is unbelievable," and "I love Americans." He left gift baskets in our rooms and set us up with a driver for the weekend. What more could he offer her? I gave the table a knock-knock.

"Hello Rita," I voiced. "What's Trish talking about?"

Trish's eyes got wide as she downed a glass.

"Well I know it's only been like a month...." Rita was now flushed head to toe. "But Robert has asked me to move in with him and stay in England after our contract is up. I told him I would need to get past the new year, especially with Jack and he understands."

"But don't be daft," Trish interjected. "He's loaded .... In his bank and his pants from what I hear."

Lynn giggled and chimed in, "The company will offer you a permanent role in month four. Probably sooner since you both are rolling through this start-up ahead of schedule."

My head shot to Lynn with a stunned expression.

"They don't move people for temporary projects unless they think they are worth it to relocate," she continued with a shrug. "It's just to lessen the shock factor. Why do you think they are so generous with the salary upfront? No other companies would give per diem, food and board, childcare, and increased salary."

I sat back dumbfounded. I had landed in so many traps moving here. Rita rubbed my arm with a one-sided smile. "I'm seriously so happy for you Rita," I told her. "Robert seems amazing – and uncomplicated. Cheers."

We all raised our glasses and Trish let out a cackle. "You do have the corner on complications, Mel," she said as we clinked.

"Ugh – no kidding," I grumbled. "I mean I don't think I deserve to be happy anyway. I'll be left with no one at the end of this. Right where I have been for six years. Where I belong."

"Don't get all depressed drunk," Lynn slurred. "You deserve all the dick." She clanked her glass with mine once more.

"Right," Lynn frowned. "You had a husband who bonked someone else. Then the bloke up and dies on you. Left with a baby. Why are you so hard on yourself? You deserve a million pounds and all the wine in the world. Oh look – here's the wine."

I smiled softly and twirled a glass in my hands. They all glared at me in unison waiting for my response.

"Because she killed her husband," a voice boomed from behind us.

What the fuck?

"Not your conversation bi-atch," Rita shouted over my head.

"Bye!"

I turned around ready to smack some drunk idiot. A stunning woman sauntered over to us. She had on stilettos and diamond jewelry. A tan wrap dress accented her bronzed skin and black hair. She walked with such confidence she couldn't possibly be smashed - unlike my entourage.

"In most countries, goodbye means leave," I spat her direction. As she came closer, I could feel the tingles on the back of my neck. My skin prickled and I instinctively stood to meet her gaze.

A cruel smile crossed her lips as she shifted to one hip. The slit in her dress exposed a perfectly toned thigh. *Bitch.*

Trish stepped in front of me waving a glass in her face. "I didn't know there was whore offered on this boat. What's your going rate now?"

The woman looked down at her nails as if she was bored. "Classic quip, Patricia. How do you manage?"

"With great girlfriends that would prefer you to leave."

"Aren't you going to introduce me? Perhaps I need no introduction – Carmela, is it? Well, Carmela, I'm Claudia, and if anyone is unwanted as of late, it's you."

CHAPTER 31

It's funny the things you think about in crisis situations, and this definitely qualified as a crisis. Things like - How far down is that water? Is white linen see-through when wet? Why does Paul's wife resemble an exotic supermodel? And once again, will Scotland yard arrest us for whatever is about to transpire?

"Oh, don't look so sick, Mel," Claudia shot at me. "This is the part where you say "pleasure to meet you," or some similar lie. Maybe you could tell me why, in two weeks, my husband has admitted to having an emotional affair with you and then moved in with you."

Without thinking, and I couldn't blame them, all the ladies turned their eyes to me. "He's not living with me," I countered. "He moved to Winlin and I didn't even know. I haven't responded to his messages."

"But you did. You told him you would be here." *Shit. I did tell him I was coming here and to give me some time.*

"And now you are here. So - you are intercepting his texts?"

"He's my husband and I'll check his messages and email and whatever else I damn well please."

Trish chirped in, "Impeccable marriage advice. I'll park that for the future."

"And what would you know about anything Patricia? Future with who – a barfly?" Trish hated to be called Patricia and I could feel her anger rising every time she heard Claudia say it. I could see our nervous sommelier in the distance. He caught wind of our argument and was chatting with other employees.

I stepped into the space between Trish and Claudia. "I don't know what you wanted to accomplish here. I'm not seeing Paul. I didn't – I didn't come here for him. It's not like that."

"Maybe that's true. From what I hear you don't know who you came here for, or who is making you come, rather? Sleeping with Milo already? No surprise there – who hasn't. But it's a good thing you won't be here very long. He bores easily once he's caught his prey."

Rita and Lynn inhaled a sharp breath. I saw someone from the crew tap on Lynn's shoulder. This disaster was about to unfurl.

Claudia stepped closer. "You think you are the only woman to be chased by Milo Bennett. It's a sport for him. We all had a turn," she whispered harshly, darting her eyes to Trish. If Trish opened her mouth at that moment, I was sure fire would spit out. "But you aren't one to judge for past mistakes, are you? Murderers aren't that type."

Two gentlemen from the crew stepped on either side of Claudia. She let out an irritated breath. She had much more to say I was sure. "I'm leaving," she said to them. Lifting her finger to my face once more she spat, "Why don't you ask Milo for a list of all his corporations, especially the subsidiaries? You may be surprised how much control he has inside and outside the bedroom. Especially when it comes to international placements. Do you think you know the secrets he keeps from you? You haven't scratched the surface."

The crew gently pulled her away and she collected herself like an actress, flashing a smile at them as she strolled back to whatever hole she had crawled out of.

Trish was shaking with anger next to me. I was grateful she stood up for me. A member of the crew assured us we would be given unlimited flights on the house and Mrs. Masterson would not be coming to the upper level for the remainder of our voyage.

I flinched when he said Mrs. Masterson and Rita audibly groaned. We returned to our seats and I slumped in my chair. Claudia had been nasty to me, but I would have done the same in her position. I should have told her I encouraged Paul to concentrate on his marriage. I'm not a terrible person. I'm the last person who would condone cheating.

Trish started to silently weep at the table.

"What's going on?" I fussed at her. "Please don't – what's happening?"

"I'm so sorry," Trish cried. "It was in school. I haven't had a sexy thought about Milo in twenty years. He doesn't even look like the same person. I mean his willy I'm sure didn't change, but, oh God, why did I say that? Bloody hell – I'm so sorry."

"Wait – what?"

"We were seventeen and I got pissed one night at a party. It's a small town! The next day I think – we agreed it was awful and we wouldn't speak about it again. Oh God, I hope he's gotten better."

Lynn and Rita started laughing like hyenas. I stared at Trish in shock. As the minutes went by and their laughter continued, I couldn't help but join in. Trish thought we had all gone mad and said so. When I gained my composure, I grabbed her in a hug. Highschool hookups were the least of my worries. I knew what Claudia was trying to do, but I'm not that petty.

"I don't care that you slept with Milo as a teenager, Trish," I said. "I mean, now that I think about it, when would you have told me? I'm basically a tornado here rolling through these brothers. But let's never mention his willy again, okay?"

Trish wiped tears from her eyes. "It was half my LIFETIME ago. God that makes me feel old, but I swear I didn't even really remember. I'm that much of a whore."

"You're not!" I shrieked.

"Thank you, Mel," she continued. "But am I out of line to ask what she was talking about with all the murder bullshit?"

My face fell and my breathing stopped.

"Or not," Lynn chimed in. "We don't need to know shit. In fact, you keep this wine coming. We won't even know who we are or who we slept with, like Trish here."

I chuckled at her joke, and my body relaxed. I was just drunk enough and my give-a-fuck meter was just low enough to confess. That's what it was - a confession - one I hadn't spoken to anyone.

Maybe I hadn't said the words, but I had written them.

Milo knew and loved me, maybe they would too.

CHAPTER 32

Dear Paul,

October 18th, 2014

Today was Mitch's funeral. To everyone that has asked, I've said crap like – It was beautiful – It brought closure – We are so honored

LIES - It was awful.

It was awful for all the expected reasons – like, you know - burying my husband sixty years before his expiration date. It was awful because my family cornered me and demanded I go to a therapist because I haven't held Eva since he died and that didn't go as unnoticed as I thought.

Postpartum isn't a thing when they are a year old, but apparently, survivors' guilt is, so I'm getting shipped off to a nuthouse. Or I am if I don't go see someone three times a week starting tomorrow, so great way to end the night.

Oh, a great way to end the night was meeting Audrey. That was the icing on this arsenic-filled cake. She came to the funeral wearing a skin-tight mid-thigh grey dress and fishnets.

SHE WORE GOD DAMNED FISHNETS PAUL.

What person not working in a nightclub or going to a Halloween party is wearing fishnets? Fine – you want to be an emo chick – how about not at a funeral. Just my opinion, but what do I know – I'm just the wife.

Or widow now.

The true gem of the evening was the story I told myself that no one would find out they had an affair. In my head, they went to school together, so she was there showing her respects.

But much to my surprise, Audrey just can't keep her mouth shut. Maybe that's how my husband's dick fell in, but how will I ever know – because he's dead.

Everyone that would listen heard the tale of their love affair. She had pictures of them kissing. You know that disgusting selfie people take? Like – hey I climbed this mountain with my boyfriend here we are kissing at the top.

It gets better.

As you know, Mitch's mom (or mum - you British weirdo), was never a big Carmela fan. She decided to go off on me asking if I ended his life support because of the affair.

Wait no – that's not right – she didn't ask. She screamed at me that I did. She called me a murderer.

She slapped me – twice. You know when you get slapped you think you will hit someone back. Not me. I just stood there like an idiot, waiting for it to happen again. Which it did!

Then my family had to cocoon me in a safe space while Mitch's family talked about me. Audrey bawled like a toddler with them. Aunt June spit at me as I left the funeral. She SPIT at me.

But you know what the worst part is Paul – the horrible truth? Maybe they should be mad at me. Maybe – just maybe – I didn't give a fuck about his life anymore. He didn't care about mine.

He didn't care about our family when he was balls deep in fishnets. He didn't think of me when he was working late five nights a week. When he had a work trip over Labor Day weekend, which was the timestamp of Audrey's smooching selfies, he wasn't thinking about my life.

All I know is when they turned off the machines, I didn't feel sad. I felt rage.

Rage at what he had done. Rage that he had left the house to get milk and bread, and for some reason, drove fifteen miles away instead of to the store at the front of our neighborhood. Rage that the receipt was at a grocer in front of Audrey's apartments. Rage that if he had been where he should have been, home with me, he would be alive right now. Rage that he didn't love me enough.

I always loved him enough, but not enough to keep those machines going.

-       Mel

P.S. I don't think saying mum instead of mom makes you a weirdo – but why – just why?

P.P.S. For a kilometer's conversion – 15 miles = too fucking far away for milk

P.P.P.S Do not make a Rage Against the Machine joke. TOO SOON.

CHAPTER 33

I told the ladies everything that night. All the ugly thoughts and feelings bubbled up as I admitted the worst thoughts and feelings about myself. Everyone cried, which signifies you've had a successful girl's trip. I think it's in the handbook somewhere.

They insisted I was not a killer which gave me some comfort. I persisted with them that the doctors gave me a choice. I could keep him on the machines or I could pull them and donate his organs. He didn't have brain activity, but his family insisted he should remain in a facility. He would miraculously wake up one day according to them. I led them to believe this is what he wanted – that we had talked about it. Lie – that conversation never happened.

Still, the women kept their stance on our way home and into late-night conversations. In their view, I was an innocent victim of lying, deceiving, manipulative men. The drunk driver was even a man. Fuck all those men – except for Robert who was wonderful and putting us up in his home.

In the morning Rita was lying in bed with me, holding my hand. I sat up to see black and tan smudges on the pristine white pillow -

a combination of never removing my makeup and crying all night. There was an empty wine bottle on the floor, dripping red liquid on a grey rug. Robert should have gotten a damage deposit.

I groaned as I peeled myself out of the bed, my head pounding, and shuffled into the kitchen.

"Morning," I mumbled to Lynn and Trish. They squealed like they had seen a ghost and dropped papers all over the floor. I pushed my fingertips to my temples. "What the hell? I'm dying here. Why is every light on in here?"

Trish started collecting loose sheets that fell across the kitchen floor. I saw a picture of Milo that had slid to my feet. "What the fuck?" I grumbled raising my arms in the air.

They gave each other a devious look. "So, you may have forgotten in the whirlwind of a night involving the angry soon-to-be ex-wife, murder confession, and vineyard of grapes, but Claudia accused Milo of tricking you to move to England," Trish said.

"With his businesses," Lynn continued.

"Which are in these background checks," Trish screeched.

"You are going through my things," I accused, walking through the house turning lights off.

"We are not," Trish said. "You brought these files out last night amid our man-bashing. They were still on the counter this morning, practically begging to be read."

"Shit I did do that." I slowly sat on a barstool and laid my pounding head on the cold granite. "Well did you find anything?"

They both nodded in unison. I remained head down and held out my hand. "Give it here."

Lynn sat next to me and lowered her face to my level. She slid a few pages my way. "Difficult to read sideways chick, so I'll sum it up. Milo owns Winlin Investments, which we assumed was only rental properties. But it's a parent company to several subsidiaries. One of which is Outreach Partners."

My head lifted at that. Outreach Partners was the seed money for my consulting agency. They vested seventy-five percent of the Prometheus Project.

"It gets better," Lynn kept on. "Do you know who is the president of Outreach Partners?"

"Oh yeah," I said. "Absolutely."

They gave each other a questioning look.

"No - I don't fucking know," I snapped. "This isn't Forensic Files. It's like you all are enjoying dragging this out."

Lynn patted my arm and rolled her eyes. "You are ruining my fun. Warner Masterson — Milo's father."

"His father is in a home," I said. "He can't be …." The puzzle pieces started clicking together. Outreach had never invested in our startups before. We have a shortlist that we work with internationally, but Outreach was brimming with cash up front. Money talks. How many letters did I write dreaming that I could start fresh in another place - on a new project — maybe a dozen.

"That son of a bitch. He funded Prometheus and named you to run the project," Lynn said.

"Uhhhhh does that make him a son of a bitch or a hopeless romantic?" Trish asked. "I get that I'm the only one that has known Milo my whole life. A little too intimately I admit – sorry about that Mel."

"Please stop bringing it up," I grumbled.

"Anyway," she asserted. "He is enamored with you. I'm telling you, the past ten years, no other woman stuck around. Like Claudia alluded, I'm sure he had his fair share of shagging, but he's been pining for you. He's bloody loaded. There are far more nefarious ways to get you here."

At that moment, Rita let out a blood-curdling scream from the living room. *Oh my God, my head.*

We scurried to her as she was gagging into an empty trash can. She was not handling the hangover very well from what I could see.

Rita sat on her knees and pointed towards the front door covering her mouth like it might projectile at any moment.

"What is it?" I demanded making my way to the door.

The smell hit me first. Rotting meat and putrid sulfur filled my nostrils and I understood Rita's reaction. The walkway to Robert's front door was lined in dead rodents and fish. Shit - I hope Robert got some kind of insurance policy for this weekend.

"What – What is this?" I stammered. My hands covering my nose and mouth from the stench.

"This," Trish squeaked from a pinched nose. "Is Claudia Masterson."

CHAPTER 34

It took two hours for us to clean up the walkway and the bloody CHEATER written on the front door. Well not entirely true. It took two hours for us to give up and call Robert with apologies and cries for help.

It's interesting how money can change your outlook on big problems. In one moment, I'm wailing on a manicured lawn about animal entrails, and the next, Robert has us all at a spa getting massages.

He hired half a dozen men to clean up and stand guard at the house. His security footage didn't show much. It looked to be a few teenagers in head-to-toe black, but we all knew who was really behind the Carrie remake.

We had four massage tables in the dimly lit room. Sounds of rainwater and ocean tides played with the occasional grunt from a released muscle. I alternated between moments of relaxation and complete panic. I preferred the spa to the carnage we left behind, but my problems followed me here, filling my head.

The question had to come at some point from one of the ladies, and it was Rita who ripped off the band-aide.

"Do you know what are you going to do when we get back?"

"Well I'm giving a generous donation to P.E.T.A. for one," I smirked. The room filled with giggles. When it quieted, I felt their eyes on me.

I cleared my throat. "I'm having dinner with Paul."

Rita sat up and her sheet fell down. The male masseuse turned on his heel quick to look away. "Paul – not Milo? Or just Paul first?"

My back muscles had tightened completely back up reversing all the work this poor girl had just done. "I need to defuse the Claudia situation. It just needs to get sorted out with him first."

"Why do you care about Claudia?" Trish said. "She's a treacherous whore. She does not fight fair. You need to be careful with her."

Her antics hit below the belt, but she hadn't been wrong. Trish had sex with Milo - half a lifetime ago - but it happened. Milo did have connections to my company and the reason I'm here. I had made the decision, but he had influence. I still thought about the letters after Mitch died. I begged for an escape hatch. *Did I push him to do this for me?*

From Claudia's perspective, was I a homewrecker? I had read the letters Paul wrote and never sent a dozen more times. I didn't know how I felt about them yet. *Would I know when I saw him?*

"I texted him when we were in the waiting room," I confessed. "I just said that we would be home tomorrow and I wanted to meet for dinner and talk. I didn't tell him about the Claudia stuff."

I left it at that, but the room was deadly silent. Even the masseuses were frozen waiting for what happened next.

"Aaaaand," Trish groaned waving her hand.

"I haven't checked my phone but I imagine he agreed since he moved to my neighborhood to chase me down and you know – all the love confessions."

I heard feet patter on the floor.

"Jesus woman, you are in your knickers," Trish cackled.

Rita had leaped from the table and was rifling through my bag in the corner. This poor spa employee. He just faced the wall with his head in his hands. She then startled me, tilting my face to unlock the phone.

Before I could protest, she started reading.

I'm so glad to hear from you. Relieved beyond belief, Mel. I know you heard I moved to Winlin. I don't want to scare you off, but I have to be more forceful. You need to know how I feel with more than words. Come to my house for dinner, please. As soon as you can. 17 Winlin.

"Yikes he's a house or two away from me," Trish uttered.

"Yikes he wants you to come over so he can seduce you and fuck you all night," Rita pointed out.

"Yikes you are standing in the middle of the room in your panties, Rita," Lynn yelled. "This poor man has been staring at the wall for twenty minutes and all he wants to do is rub your feet. Put your ass back on the table."

More laughing filled the room and even the employees of the spa were snickering. Rita returned to her table with an apology and promised to keep herself covered for the remainder of our forty minutes. Lynn suggested we spend the rest of our time enjoying our massage in silence and I was grateful.

When we came back to Robert's house that evening, not a speck of the bloodshed could be found. Dinner had been ordered in and I avoided any Milo or Paul talk for the evening - even when Milo texted me Goodnight, Beautiful just as he had the night before. I was in more of a man-bashing mood then, but now it gave me a twinge of guilt. You are not cheating because A) you are not in a relationship with Milo and B) it's just dinner with Paul.

The worry was in the back of my mind all evening. I joined in girl talk and joked and played games, but every other thought came back to the same question.

Could I really just have dinner with Paul?

CHAPTER 35

I had agreed to meet with Paul on Wednesday. Monday would be a nightmare after a long weekend and I wanted a night with the kids Tuesday. Weeknights are safer. I'm less likely to turn into a whore on a school night.

I had started Wednesday with positive thoughts. I was even using the bus this week. Milo was not. Rita pointed out he likely never needed to use it. He just wanted to see me.

When I entered my office that morning, all those happy vibes flew out the window. The entire place was in chaos. No one was sitting down and suits from the executive floors were pacing through the aisles. *What the fuck?*

Rita and I stood with our mouths gaped open, unsure of what to do. Lynn came over red-faced and disheveled.

"What – what?" I said making some circular motions with my hands around the office.

"Have you been able to check your email from your phone?" Lynn spat.

"No. It hasn't been working all morning."

"FUCKING EXACTLY," Lynn screamed back. Her ponytail whipped around her head as she did a small jump. "Everything is down. The whole server room is fried. The entire IT department is just standing in front of it like they spotted a damn UFO or something. No one can log in or do shit. Settle in ladies - today is going to suck."

She threw her hands up in the air and walked towards the group of tech folks pacing around our server room. "Is this a Goddamn Star Trek convention? Work the problem."

Rita held my arm and leaned close. "She's going to eat them alive," she whispered.

"No kidding," I said and started towards our offices. "You know we are still ahead. This isn't as terrible for us."

"Oh no – your dinner with Paul. Do you think you can still go?" Rita asked.

I shrugged my shoulders as we stepped into the middle conference room. A giant sheet of paper on the table had a message written in red marker.

Main conference room at 9:30. Bring any project plan paper files you have or maybe just your brain until we can function like the 21st century. Rebuilding the timeline from scratch.

"No," I said deadpan. "I don't think I'll be going."

Paul wasn't happy with my cancelation.

I texted him at first because I'm a coward and he called immediately. He didn't seem to believe me until he heard Lynn screaming at a group of interns about crisis management in the background.

He offered to bring dinner to me, but there was no point. Stopping to eat and talk would just drag the night out longer. We had to wheel in a dozen whiteboards and map out our project plan and completed deliverables.

There is nothing more infuriating than being thrust into group projects. It's one of my worst high school memories and here we are - a million years later - reliving the nightmare.

It was a nice boost to my ego that Rita and I are some of the few with our shit together. I was praying we could be excused after our part, but we had to "get through this together" - direct quote from the People Team. Misery loves company.

Nearing midnight, a line of cars started to pick up groups in front of our building. Another thirty minutes of waiting for a ride plus the commute home meant I wasn't in my house until well after one in the morning. The servers were still down and interns were bringing in sleeping bags when I left. It would be another long day tomorrow.

The kids were excited to have a sleepover at Mrs. MacArthur's. They had comfy clothes to sleep in and toiletries, but she said they were out of school clothes. I wasn't sure if Rita or I would wake up in time, so I started collecting things to walk over and leave on her porch for the morning. *More flowers with her groceries again.*

Shuffling around my house, I started tossing the kids things in a box, cursing under my breath. Work had been the one thing going right, and now I was dreading it.

Footsteps? Is Milo awake?

I grabbed the box and started out of my door. *It's the middle of the night. He's probably just getting a drink of water or something.*

I didn't even make it to the street when I heard the slam of the door behind me. His steps were soft and I turned when I felt him right behind me.

He had been sleeping. He had on sweatpants, a wrinkled shirt, and his hair was tousled. Sexy as fuck and I felt my skin prickle at the sight of him.

"You don't have any shoes on," I mumbled.

"I thought I wouldn't catch you if I stopped to get them," he said, stepping closer.

I took a step back. Milo's brows scrunched. He had a hurt expression. I had texted him back Good Night this week and told him I was busy until the weekend, but that had been the most of it since we were both together last.

He had texted more than once that he would see me this weekend. He wanted confirmation I hadn't given, and now I was backing away from him. I didn't trust myself with him. I couldn't clear up anything with Paul if I kept falling in bed with Milo. *But God it's tempting.*

"It's late and you shouldn't walk alone," he said. "Where are you going?"

"I need to drop off school clothes to Mrs. MacArthur. She has the kids," I explained.

"Let me walk with you. Or let me drop them off for you."

I thought on it a moment - standing in the cold dark. It would be a good time to pry for more information. *Lies I tell myself to be close to him.* "Get some shoes," I said.

He jogged inside and was back out a moment later with shoes in his hands. He sat on the steps to put them on and then held his hands out for the box. I started down the street and had an evil thought.

"I heard you slept with Trish," I announced with a smirk. Milo tripped on the pavement and the box tumbled a little. He looked over at me with wide eyes and a shocked expression. I gave a wicked smile, not ready to put him out of his misery.

"Yes, I s-s-suppose that happened. Twenty or so years ago," he answered. "We were in school and it was just once. I t-t-think we were both smashed at the time."

I held my hand up for him to stop. "I'm messing with you a bit, but it's a good ice breaker, right?"

"I'm so sorry," he said.

"You don't need to be sorry for that, Milo. I was just kidding around. I'm pretty sure Trish forgot."

"Oh well that's nice," he winced.

"I think that's more because Trish is Trish, not because you are you," I said putting my hand on his shoulder. His skin was hot and I had to pull it away before I got too close.

"I do have some questions still," I whispered. He was silent, ready for me to start.

"Trish also said you haven't had a relationship in ten years. Is that true?"

"Yes, that's true. Maybe a while longer," he answered.

I gave my thighs some light slaps as we walked. This man could not expand on a thought unless forced.

"Okay so why is it that you are the eternal bachelor yet now you are moving at lightning speed with, you know – like you seem to want…."

"You," he said. "I want to be with you."

I looked down at my feet as we walked. We were at Mrs. MacArthur's steps. In a few leaps, he was at her front door and set the box in one of her rocking chairs and we started back.

"That question seems redundant, Mel," he said, looking at me as we walked. I could feel my skin flush and my breath quicken. "If you want me to say it, I'm happy to. I wanted you all those years. I don't want to get into a discussion about women that I dated, but their intentions weren't always respectable. I do quite well …. financially and that seemed to be what they were interested in more than me. You aren't like that."

"Right, because I didn't even know who you were," I clipped.

His shoulders rose and his jaw tightened. "I deserve that, but you are different. You know who I am at my core – who was writing to you."

We walked in silence for a bit. I wasn't ready to show my cards about the move to London just yet, but I had other questions he needed to answer. I stopped walking and turned to him.

191

"Why did you sleep with me knowing you were lying to me? How could you hurt me like that – knowing everything I've been through." My breath caught and I fought back tears. Heat shot up my neck and I felt my eyes water.

"Because I'm selfish," his voice cracked. He cleared his throat and started again. "I had to have you – before Paul. I'm a selfish bugger that wanted to be close to you - in every way. Have I fucked it all up, Mel?"

I shook my head no. I couldn't deny my feelings for him. He pulled me into his arms and brought his lips to mine. I opened my mouth and let his tongue meet mine. His hands moved under my shirt and up my back. His grip moved around to my ribs and then thrust me away from him. My breath left my lungs and I was flushed and confused.

"What's wrong?" I sputtered.

"I don't want to keep things from you. I won't do that again, so I need to talk to you about today," he said.

My face crumpled in confusion. I opened my mouth to speak, but no words escaped. Milo kept his grip on my waist but didn't meet my gaze.

"Your company had a server crash today," he continued. "I know something about it. I – I have some interest in your company. I have some interest in your contracts in London."

Shit. He was going to confess. Play dumb.

"My family owns Outreach Partners," he confessed. "I did promise to fund every bid that had your name as a project manager. You should know that. I own several companies so it's

192

not as outlandish as you may think. I'm not trying to be a braggart, just give perspective about the situation. But I won't keep it from you that I wanted you here and I did what I could to get you here without telling you. I – I didn't want you to think you didn't deserve it you see. You were already listed as a potential project manager when we entered contracts. I didn't request you – you earned this on your own – understand?"

I was silently nodding as he spoke. I didn't respond, afraid to give myself away. He gently massaged my bare waist and pulled me closer. His explanation didn't seem completely out of reach. *Although, all I'm thinking about is his dick inside me – wonder if that's clouding my judgment.*

He swallowed hard and continued, "I crashed the servers."

I released from his grip with a start. I just had a sixteen-hour day because he crashed the fucking servers. Work was the only thing giving me peace and he crashed the fucking servers! *Why?*

"What – what – what the fuck?" I stammered.

He took a deep breath and his chest expanded and tightened against his shirt. "It's hard to explain."

Sudden clarity came over me and then rage took its place. He was manipulative, to say the least, but intelligent and had his pulse on everything I had been and would be doing. It wasn't hard to explain - it was hard to come clean.

"You sabotaged my dinner with Paul," I shrieked. "Of all the insecure, ridiculous things to do. You can't control everything, Milo. I will see him. You can't keep doing this. What's next, huh? You move my job to Brazil and suddenly show up there?"

"No – n-n-no," he stuttered. "I knew about that, but that's not why...."

"Why would I believe you? You're a liar," I yelled starting back to my house. His steps were right behind me. "Stop following me, Milo. I'm texting Paul when I get inside and meeting him tomorrow even if you set my fucking building on fire."

"I live here - I'm not following. Please, Mel. I promise I'm being honest. That's not what happened."

I was in a full jog when I made it to my steps. He was right behind me, repeating my name - which I ignored.

I slammed the blue door behind me and swept my key into my lock - opening the door quickly. I turned to shut it behind me and Milo was standing in the entryway.

"Please, Mel," he started, but I didn't give him the chance.

I slammed the door in his face and grabbed my phone from my pocket.

> *Sorry it's late Paul, but I'll see you tomorrow night*
> *– your house*

CHAPTER 36

Paul's house wasn't much different from the others in Winlin - slightly bigger with an extra room that was in use as an office. It was either fully furnished or he had moved quickly. Everything was in its place and decorated. It didn't scream bachelor pad, so that was a plus. The smell was amazing. Something Italian I would guess and he had wine glasses ready on the table.

I was beyond uncomfortable. There is being on edge or being uneasy and then there was me – crawling out of my skin and ready to run all the way back to America.

The workday had been never-ending. There wasn't much Rita or I could do without any technology except sit in a large room of whiteboards and question our life decisions. I didn't dare tell her that Milo was responsible for our misery. She would track him down and choke him to death.

After about ten hours of deliberating how dinner would go tonight and still no restored servers, I called it and announced our departure. Rita shot everyone a peace sign as we strutted off the floor. We were still ahead while everyone else was falling more and more behind. I could feel the daggers shooting at the back of my skull. Considering the whole mess was my fault, I deserved them.

"I'm really glad you agreed to see me again." Paul sighed, completely at ease. He walked around the kitchen to check a few things and then gave an ample pour to the glasses. His mannerisms reminded me of Milo and my heart picked up the pace.

The way he smiled out of one side of his mouth. The way he would run his hand through his hair. The way he would reach for my face to brush his thumb on my cheek. *Whoa – stop.*

I took a step back and pulled his touch away. It felt familiar and foreign in a way that made me light-headed. I grabbed a glass and had a generous sip.

"I made lasagna," Paul said with a smirk, grabbing his glass. "I know it was your favorite and I love it. I hope you still like it." He started grabbing things out of the cabinets and refrigerator for our meal. Parmesan and plates – another bottle of wine.

I took a seat at the kitchen table. "That sounds nice," I agreed.

"Did you read all the letters? The notebook?"

"No never got around to it," I scoffed.

Paul's eyes got wide for a moment and then softened. "You always had that sarcastic streak. How did they make you ... feel – I guess."

I took another gulp of liquid courage. "The short answer is I don't know, but we need to circle back to your wife. A few weeks ago, you were going to talk her into meeting me, and now you left her. Red flags much?"

Paul gave me a sideways smile. "Did you want to meet Claudia – really?"

"Well now I have."

He slammed the oven door and shot me a look. "Oh God, what did she do?"

"She yelled at me on a boat about being a husband thief – possibly true. Also, about being a murderer – still up in the air on that one. Oh, and Milo is a big man-whore too, she says. There's also a strong possibility she unloaded a truck of dead rodents on Robert's front lawn."

Paul's mouth was ajar and he reached for the counter with one hand. He kept opening his mouth to speak but no words came out for a minute or two. Taking a few steps towards me he pulled out a chair and sat by my side. "I'm so sorry, Mel. She can be – irrational. Crazy."

"Yeah, so women don't like to be called crazy, and about that, maybe she isn't. I can see her point of view. I've been the one screwed over before. Remember?"

"I'm not having a secret affair. This is different."

"It's all deception," I argued. My skin felt hot. He was rationalizing lies. "Why did you leave your wife, Paul?"

He reached for me again and I moved the chair back with a screech on the floor. A deflated expression covered his face as he set his arms on the table. "You aren't the reason, but you are the catalyst. She has broken every vow there is, and that doesn't cover half of it. We haven't slept in the same bed for years, Mel. I mean it when I say this is different."

Years - they haven't slept in the same bed.

Paul said everything as a matter of fact. No feeling in his voice, just relaying information. He didn't love her anymore. "Did she cheat on you?"

"Many times," he hissed. "She claims she slept with Milo."

My heart exploded in my chest. Heat filled my face and my expression hardened. Paul bit the inside of his cheek at my response. He looked down at his hands and continued. "She didn't. The dates don't line up. She claimed they were somewhere I know he wasn't. That's one of Claudia's talents. She's devious. She will do anything to get what she wants. Tear apart families."

"Well thanks for the warning, but you know, I'm not helping with the Masterson family togetherness either."

"That's not on you, Mel. But please know she doesn't want me or our marriage anymore. I'm not sure she ever did. She wants money, but mine is locked up. My brothers have the key and she signed a prenup. She'll want to … discredit you - us. It may give her an edge to dispute the prenup. I'm sorry. Just be careful."

"I keep hearing that." I pushed my chair back to the table, crossed my legs, and waited for him to continue. He's an open book compared to Milo. *Stop thinking about Milo.*

"I stayed because of Nina. And the only other woman I ever wanted was you. I'm – I'm …. very upset about Milo. He's not the man for you. He's never had a serious relationship. He doesn't know what it's like to lose a marriage. We do. He didn't tell me you were even moving here. I found out by chance two days before."

The timer for dinner pinged and Paul groaned, annoyed at the break in the conversation. I got up to help set the table. Everything looked delicious and it was sweet that he cooked. Lasagna wasn't my favorite anymore, but I wouldn't hurt his feelings. Good food is still good food.

"I need to know what you thought about the letters – the book," Paul asked again before we took our first bite.

"Confused..." I pushed my food around my plate and took a big bite to buy myself some time while he waited. "Do you remember when you were supposed to come to Maine? That summer your mom died."

"I still regret not going." Paul's voice had a solemn tone. "I didn't have another opportunity – not like Milo – and I just always thought I would."

"At that time, I was crazy in love with you. I was sure if you came to America, I would fall head over heels. But you didn't and then you met Claudia in school and...," my voice drifted off. "Maybe Milo had the opportunity but he didn't take it."

Paul's eyes darted from his plate to mine and he shifted in his chair. He put his hand on top of mine and met my gaze. "I would have never looked back, Mel. I would have been with you forever from that moment, and I knew it. I was scared. Finding your forever at eight years old, it just seemed unreal. I knew if I went, I would be .... stuck maybe. That's the wrong word, but maybe at eighteen that's how it felt."

"I get that. I'm just saying that's what changed everything." I pulled my hand from him to eat. We continued like that for a while – in silence.

"Do you remember the summer after university?" Paul added. "The summer you decided you would settle for Mitch?"

I dropped my fork on my plate with a small clang. No one had ever said it out loud – the truth of what Mitch and I were. "I don't think that's very fair Paul," I sneered. "We had a history and I loved Mitch. I did love him. He wasn't perfect and I'm realizing I'm about as far from perfect as one can be."

"You decided out of fear, Mel."

"And you didn't?" I snapped.

"Yes, I fucking did. You broke my heart and every choice since has been in an effort to protect it."

Tears pricked my eyes and I stared at my plate, full of anger and grief. The past couldn't be undone. I was here to face it, but that was easier said than done.

We resumed eating with only the sound of silverware hitting the plates. The silence was deafening and it took everything in me not to bolt.

"Does this count as a date?" Paul asked giving a wink. He could feel how uncomfortable this was too and wanted to stop the bleeding.

"Uh – I don't know." The thought flashed in my brain - *I'm sleeping with your brother.* I remembered Milo's mouth on my most sensitive areas and my face turned red.

"Don't be embarrassed. I want to date you. I mean, I would like to take you out on a proper date."

The idea was tempting. In all the encounters with Milo, he had never asked to make a meal for me or date me. Maybe Claudia had a point about him winning a prize. *Would he be done with me if he championed over Paul?*

"Let me think about it, okay?" I replied still blushing.

"Okay," Paul clipped. His shoulders stiffened. "When Nina was born, I told myself we could never happen. I had to convince myself to let it go. Would you have stayed with Mitch after what he did – for Eva?"

A lump grew in my throat. I knew I would have stayed, and I hated how weak it made me. It would mean Paul was weak too. Both of us doing what's comfortable. That's what Paul felt to me, comfortable.

"Yes. I had decided to work it out before his accident. I guess I – I didn't decide really. It was assumed."

"This is a fresh start for both of us," he pleaded, reaching his hand to my cheek. He leaned closer to me and cupped my face. I tilted into his embrace and exhaled closing my eyes. I felt his lips first, soft and gentle. Then his hand around the back of my neck pulling us closer.

Calmness washed over my body as I ran my hands through his hair and he lifted me to his lap. I was straddling him as he reached his hand under my ass moving me to feel him, how hard he was for me.

Tingles started between my legs and washed over my body. He kissed with gentle pressure – lightly reaching his tongue to massage mine. His lips never left my skin, but there wasn't aggression or pushing. It felt intimate and caring.

He reached his hand down the opening in the back of my pants, cupping my bare ass and pushing me harder into him.

Stop, Mel, Stop.

I snaked my hands to his chest and pushed - gently breaking our kiss. His eyes darted from my eyes to my breasts and further down. It made me shudder knowing what he was thinking. What we were both thinking?

"Paul - I have to go," I breathed. "I can't do this. I'm not this type of woman."

He was still gently rocking my body over his length quietly panting. I placed a hand on his knee behind me to still him. "Stop, Paul – we can't."

"But Milo can," he hissed. His words felt like a bullet to the gut.

"Don't ruin this before it starts," I snapped rising from the chair.

Paul grabbed my forearms. "I'm sorry. Mel – I'm sorry." I stilled as he kept his grip on me. "So - it could start?"

"Your marriage would need to end first. Shit - that's not me telling you to end your marriage. I just – I needed to see you and talk to you. Now I need to go."

"Will you see Milo?"

I stared at him, transfixed in his question. He released my arms and I crossed them in front of my body. "Paul, I live next to him, so it's a hard question to answer."

He parted his lips to speak again and I held my hand up to stop him. "Please let's not talk about Milo. We needed to talk about us and we did. Now I need to go."

He conceded, packed some lasagna for me, and we stepped out onto the porch so I could walk home.

"Thanks for dinner, Paul, and for being so open with me. Just give me some time to think about everything. I'll think about the date."

There was another silence between us. Paul walked with me towards the street. "I don't want to leave you," he pleaded.

"I'm right down the street," I joked. My attempt to lighten the mood fell flat. "It's best I leave. We both know it."

Paul snaked his arm around my waist and pulled me into him again. He kissed me and I let him, his tongue finding his way into my mouth as I palmed his chest. I lightly pushed away but with no real strength. This time was forceful. He grabbed the back of my hair and my mouth opened in response. His hand clutching my ass almost lifting me off the cement. His cock so hard on my stomach I could feel it pulse. When he pulled away, I was almost shaking with need in his arms.

"Remember that, Mel," he teased. "While you are thinking things over."

CHAPTER 37

Text messages started at four in the morning, which was incredibly annoying since I hadn't gotten to sleep until after midnight. The servers were back up and all hands needed to be on deck. We were thankfully one of the last teams to be picked up based on our project status, but that still meant a car was coming at six.

Problem one was we couldn't get ahold of Mrs. MacArthur. It was the crack of dawn and we didn't give her notice the night before. Fifteen minutes to pick up, I started to get desperate. Rita had come over with coffee and took it as a sign that we – or she – would just have to go in later.

"Something's not right," I insisted. "I get it's early, but she's always up by now. I'm just going to walk down. Hold the car when it comes."

Rita grimaced and nodded. "Go on then. Why don't you jog if you are so keen on getting to work for no good reason at this unholy hour?"

She had been kidding, but only a few steps on the street and I was in a jog, then a sprint. My insides churned and I thought I might get sick. Why wasn't she answering? *This is just a panic attack because of what has been going on lately. You are deflecting, Mel.*

I banged on the door. "Mrs. MacArthur," I yelled. "Please just tell me you are alright." I tried to peek in the windows, but the curtains were drawn. I banged again. No answer.

After a few panicked minutes, I was pushed to the side by Milo. He had a huge ring of numbered keys and had her door opened in under a minute.

"Mrs. MacArthur," he bellowed and rushed in. We both stopped short of a few steps inside. She was lying on her side on the floor, a cup of tea spilled beside her.

"Oh my God," I cried. We shot over to her and Milo felt her neck.

"She has a pulse. Call 999," he ordered.

"The tea is still warm," I choked out, fumbling with the phone. "She hasn't been here long."

"She'll be fine," Milo insisted.

He couldn't possibly know that. He wanted me to calm down and stop crying, but I was beyond that now. I could barely speak to the operator and he had to rip the phone from me while I sobbed over her, holding her hand.

Emergency services came quickly and I called Rita while I was in the car with Milo, following. Her cracked voice on the other end of the line started the waterworks again. Rita was not someone who showed weakness easily and I knew she was broken at the thought of losing Mrs. MacArthur. When I asked her if she was okay, she could barely whisper, "I just love her so much, Mel."

It was seven hours in the hospital before a doctor came to speak with us. At that point, Trish had joined us along with Rita. She had asked if Robert could be with the kids for a few hours so she could come by and I agreed. The doctor explained that Mrs. MacArthur had a mild stroke. We reached her so quickly she should have minimal effects, but she needed to rest and stay in the hospital. We could go back and see her for a moment, but he warned us that she was heavily medicated.

Milo held my hand as we walked through the bright white hallway. The sounds of the machines triggered my memory of Mitch and our time in the hospital. I shook the thoughts away and squeezed his hand harder.

"It's alright love – I'm here," he said, kissing my forehead.

Mrs. MacArthur was awake when we entered her room, but loopy. She had a soft smile, and I didn't see any droop on either side of her face. I didn't know a lot about strokes, but I remembered that was a side effect.

Rita and I went to either side of her bed. A nurse in the room approached Trish and Milo, "You both wait outside for a moment. Not very spacious in here you see. Let's take it two at a time."

They both nodded and Milo wrapped his arm around my shoulders. "I'll be right outside." When they stepped outside, Mrs. MacArthur chuckled.

"I see you have come to your senses my dear," she laughed.

"Um not really," I replied. "I still don't have my life together. I don't even know how Milo is here or was there I guess."

"He's probably got a tracker on you, Mel. It's a plausible explanation," Rita declared.

I shook my head and moved my attention to Mrs. MacArthur. "How are you feeling? What can I do for you? I'll water your plants and check on your house."

"I just always knew you would end up together. I started to wonder if I would live to see the day. Cutting it close now, love," she continued.

She was still going on about Milo. "Let's not worry about that now," I remarked. "You have enough on your plate and I shouldn't add to it. We've put too much on you with the kids."

"I love those lambs," she exclaimed. "Don't think I'm not on duty the second I'm out of here. And I'll worry about Milo Bennett all I want. I thought he would come back with you when he was in America. I've been waiting around ever since."

That piqued our attention. Rita made eye-contact with me and a sly smile crept across her face. Mrs. MacArthur was drugged up and loose-lipped.

"Stop it," I mouthed, but the seed had been planted.

"What trip," Rita implored. "Specifically – what trip."

"The one to see Carmela – like I just said."

Rita kept on and I sat there open-mouthed unable to stop her.

"Did Paul go to see Mel? What are your thoughts on Paul?"

"I just have a soft spot for Milo is all. But no, Paul didn't go. He tried to stop Milo, but those men do what they want. I should get some rest."

"Yes, you should," I interjected. I stood up and motioned for Rita to do the same.

"When did he go?" Rita stood but couldn't help herself.

Mrs. MacArthur didn't answer but grinned and asked for some water. Rita's phone started buzzing and I took the distraction as an opportunity to get out. I was curious, but Milo was about to come in. No doubt under duress, Mrs. MacArthur would repeat our inquisition to him.

As we exited the room Rita's phone went into overdrive. "It's work," she mumbled and stepped to the other side of the hall to check her messages.

Trish skipped into the room for her turn, but Milo was nowhere to be seen. I peered down the halls and checked my phone, but didn't see him. Rita was having a terse conversation that ended with her screaming, "Fine – twenty minutes."

"What was that?" I asked.

"Smith is all out of sorts about something he found in the server crash. He HAS to speak to only me about it."

I turned pale immediately. "W-What did he find?"

"No fucking idea," she snapped. "He has to see me in person about it and we fucking owe him so I don't have a choice."

I gave Rita a squinted glare. "Who's Smith?"

"He's the IT guy getting all the dirt for us."

I'm a terrible person. I never officially met the man Rita had subjected to our investigation and illegal use of company property. We probably still owed Smith a hooker.

"Where the fuck is Milo," Rita bellowed.

"Right here," he responded, marching down the hall. Paul was on his heels.

Fuuuuuuuuuuck

Milo came towards me and had his hand around my waist. "We are leaving," he hissed in my ear.

"Don't you want to see her?" I asked.

"I'm not leaving you with him."

"Whatever," Rita barked. "Someone, take me to the Wag so I can meet Smith. Let Trish know we are leaving."

Paul gripped Milo's arm to pull him back, but he shook it off. "Milo," he snapped. "We have some things to sort out, but you should have told me about Mrs. MacArthur - selfish prig."

Milo had his grip on me so tight I could barely keep up. Paul was steady behind us. "You've lived here fifteen minutes, Marshall. Don't act like you care about everyone now."

"Oh, that's right, you lived here three weeks longer to steal my woman."

That's all it took. One swift turn and Milo's closed fist met Paul's jaw with a snap. His blow was so hard Paul's face hit the brick of the hallway. Blood splattered the white paint as Paul pushed off the wall with his palms and came back at Milo. They were on the floor swinging as I screamed at them to stop. Security was running down the hallway as the blows continued.

"Bloody hell," Trish sighed, stepping out of the hospital room.

"I always thought this would be hot, but it just seems messy and annoying," Rita echoed.

Two burly guards split them up and started carting them down the hallway. I put my head in my hands and groaned. What did I expect? Of course, my worlds would collide.

"So, do we have to bail them out or some shit, because I don't have time for that," Rita barked. "Also, I don't care if they spend a night in jail. It might be good for them."

One of the nurses came down the hall hearing the commotion. "They won't do anything like that," she answered. "Things get hot here all the time. They will lock them in separate rooms for an hour to cool off. Then let them out one at a time."

"I have ten minutes." Rita pointed at her watch and started walking.

"Don't you think I should stay until they – umm – get out," I pleaded, chasing after her.

"Abso- fucking-lutely not," Rita shot back. "Those men are grown adults. They have their own shit which, albeit, seems all about you, but it's not all about you. Whatever happens with them will happen no matter who you are really in love with. Maybe it would have bled out in their business, or when their dad died, or when the hot girl they were mind-fucking comes to London. Who knows? But you aren't responsible for their issues. And another thing," she turned and took my chin in her hand. "You still get to

be happy, Mel. You make a choice and it breaks them apart –
that's on them. You did your time in lonely prison. Got it?"

I gave a slight nod and followed Rita out of the hospital.

CHAPTER 38

Rita hopped over the bar as we entered Winlin Wag. She wasn't going to work, but claimed free pints were a perk of the trade and gave us a round. We spotted Smith as we came in and he looked like a scared puppy. I still hadn't told Rita or Lynn about Milo crashing the servers and I was just waiting for him to explode the news all over us.

"Okay, I'm here as promised," Rita said, sliding Smith a beer. He was thin and lanky with messy blonde hair and dark-rimmed glasses.

"I thought I said I could only talk to you R-Rita," he stammered.

"Yeah about that, the thing is, I'm just going to tell my girls anyway. You might as well save me the trouble. I have a boyfriend and two kids that talked him into ice cream for dinner to deal with - so out with it."

Smith gulped and held an envelope tightly in his hands. "Well, the thing is," he mumbled. "It's kind of about Carmela. It's just I think she may be … not involved … but there's something I found about her. She's in the mix of it – the crash may have something to do..."

I was visibly sweating from nerves. Rita was too agitated with him to notice.

"For fuck's sake chug some beer and spit it out," Rita grumbled, grabbing the envelope.

"Don't open that just yet," he ordered. "Okay, so I don't know who crashed the servers, but I think I know why." His eyes darted from me to Rita. He looked at me with pity. What the hell?

"There's an email that I pulled from the data matrix," he explained. His eyes roamed thinking of a way to explain this to mere mortals. "When you send an email, it doesn't go straight to the other person. It goes through channels, trying to look for spam or viruses - lots of things. It was stuck in email purgatory." We nodded in unison. His metaphor made sense. "There was an attempt to intercept the email, but there was no way to stop it because it passed the firewalls. It's been pulled from inboxes. I think the servers were crashed because someone didn't want it going out. They needed the time to erase it. No offense, Mel, but not by you or anyone on your team. Maybe for you. This is sophisticated shit. You have a guardian angel."

I grabbed the envelope from Rita's hands, opened it, and my entire body shuddered.

It was a collage of pictures. There was a shot of me and Mitch and Eva standing in front of our house at Christmas. Then there was Mitch's coroner's report. In bold highlight was DNR signed by wife following traumatic brain injury.

Then there was a picture of me and Milo. We were outside the restaurant with my arms wrapped around his neck and his hand disappearing under my skirt. A second picture of us where I was mid-orgasm and his forearm flexed between my legs.

The last shot took me a moment to understand. It was Mitch's funeral. I was standing a few feet away from everyone in a black pantsuit and a strained expression on my face. I didn't look like a grieving wife. I looked furious. My feelings that day were on display – a mix of rage and self-loathing.

Behind me, a man in black stood apart from the crowd. Strong jaw, dark hair, and tall.

It was Milo.

Was this photoshopped? Was he there?

I knew what this email was trying to say. The years that passed in-between didn't matter to anyone who didn't know anything about me and would read this like I killed my husband for my lover. They should have put in a shot of Audrey and Mitch to truly tell the story, but the perception was reality. People would see this and hate me. I could lose my job if they connected Milo to Outreach Partners. I would certainly lose everyone's respect.

I shut the file and handed it to Rita. Trish made her way over and I directed her to take a look. "Fucking Claudia," she muttered. Smith had emptied his beer and Trish made her way to the bar to get him another.

"Thank you for this, Smith," Rita said. "Is there any reason, in particular, you are sharing this? Do you want – err – anything for your trouble?"

"Oh God n-no," Smith stuttered. "I just thought you should know. I mean, I think you both are – I don't know. You're just always nice to everyone. You are single moms and you save me a cinnamon bagel when you see there is only one left. You sit with me when I have coffee by myself in the lounge. I don't want anything."

Rita's harsh tone that had been circling all night softened. "That's probably the best thing I've heard all day. We need to find you a nice hooker."

Smith's eyes squinted and he cocked his head. "I'm g-good I think."

"Right okay, how about we just have a few more beers and pretend no one saw me like this?" I said.

"I can do that," Smith agreed. Rita shrugged her shoulders, which was a solid no, but I would take what I could get.

Rita gave me odd looks all night. She knew there was more to this. I proceeded to peel the label off every beer bottle I could as a solid use of my time. A few hours later, Rita and I were walking home and I was biting my lip wondering where to start. We strolled in silence and she followed me into the house.

"Avoiding the sugared-up kids?" I smirked.

"More like scratching an itch," she said. "Where are the files on Milo?"

"In my room. I'll get them. Why?"

"Remember what Mrs. MacArthur said – about him going to America?"

"Yes. I know what was in that picture, but she had it Photoshopped."

"Really?" Rita asked. "Just get it – just to be sure."

I grabbed the file from the bedroom. We scattered the papers between us and started sifting through. It didn't take long for me to find his passport logs.

"Here's the out of country travel," I said. "It doesn't even say where he went though. Just Heathrow to Newark – then it could have been anywhere."

Rita took the papers from my hands and pursed her lips. "He went to see you at some point. It's the only thing that makes sense. Do you remember anything about that at all?"

"Don't you think I would have remembered him, Rita? Jesus – how long ago was it anyway?"

"You're right, it was years ago. Here - October 8, 2014, was the flight into the states."

My face went pale and I felt sick to my stomach. I thought I would pass out if I wasn't already sitting down. I put my face in my hands and my elbows to my knees as the tears ran out.

"What the hell?" Rita stammered. "What's wrong? Do you remember seeing him now?"

"No," I cried. "It's just - he came. He fucking came to be there for me."

Rita shook my arm to break my face free. "What?" she said.

"It was him at the funeral. Why didn't he say anything to me? He could have even said he was Paul – I don't think I would have known. I'm so messed up Rita."

Rita set the pages back down and turned me toward her. "Hey, I think we could fill the country with the could haves and should haves, right?"

I nodded in agreement. *I can't believe he was there.*

"You haven't told us much about that funeral, just that you were humiliated and alone," Rita continued. "It's just that – this here – it shows you weren't alone completely. That's something right? He showed up for you."

I tried to smile at her. She was right, I could wallow in what could have been, but it was kind that he came.

Rita sat back and squinted her eyes. "Milo crashed the servers, didn't he?"

"Yep. He sure as hell did. I thought it was to stop my dinner with Paul because I've turned into an egomaniac."

"That bastard. That glorious, heroic, hot as fuck, bastard."

"Yes - to all of that," I agreed curling my feet underneath myself. "And before you ask, no, I don't know what I'm going to do about it."

CHAPTER 39

The next day the kids and I went up to the hospital to visit Mrs. MacArthur. She had rung and said she was feeling much better and it would lift her spirits to have visitors. Her voice was clear and coherent and I wanted to see her and talk to her.

Trish and I would normally run, but she texted that she would rather go by the hospital as well. I still had no transportation, so it worked out. We spoke in code on the way there about our discovery from the night before.

"Penny for your thoughts," I muttered as we walked into the hospital.

"I think you should be happy," she smiled and held the kid's hands down the hallway. I grunted and followed.

Mrs. MacArthur's room was full of fresh flowers and cards. The kids had drawn her a picture on the way, tracing their hands to make animals. She invited them into her bed and I nervously tried to arrange them so they wouldn't yank a wire or tube.

They talked about how much they loved school and their new

friends and I felt a rush of relief that I wouldn't have to go back to America because of a slanderous email. *Yet – she's still gunning for you.*

"There's a playground by the cafeteria dears," Mrs. MacArthur said after she noticed their fidgeting.

They squealed and Trish offered to take them for a bit before we left to have lunch.

"I'll stay with her," I murmured, shifting to get comfortable in the hospital furniture.

They skipped out and I reached for Mrs. MacArthur's hand. "How are you feeling today? You seem better."

"My body feels wonderful, but my heart – it hurts a little," she sighed.

"I'm sorry – what's going on? Should I get a nurse?"

"No dear. Milo snuck by after he was done with his time out."

I nodded. "Paul and he got into a bit of a scuffle."

She squeezed my hand. "Brothers – always a battle with them. Especially Milo and Marshall."

"Did Paul – I mean Marshall, did he visit you?"

Her smile dropped a little and she brought her hands to her lips. "No, dear. He cares for me, but it's difficult."

My face crumpled in confusion.

"I didn't think you had the whole story," she admitted. "Based on all our recent events, it's best we don't dawdle then."

"Okay," I said, crossing my arms in front of my body, ready for another blow.

"Milo is my nephew. My younger sister, much younger - Catholic family, you know – had him out of wedlock with Marshall's father." She was grinding her jaw as she told me this. It was difficult for her, like a bad mark on her perfect report card of life.

I scrunched my brows and bit my lip. I knew half of this, but not all the details – especially not who Milo's mother really was.

"They had been in love before he married Marshall's mother. A lot transpired over the years, but at the end of it, no one followed their heart until it was too late," she continued. "She tortured herself over losing the love of her life. When she fell pregnant and he didn't leave his wife, she couldn't recover – and well – she didn't survive it. She took her life when Milo was a boy. Milo's father took Milo in more out of pride than love. I should have raised him myself, but I was afraid that would make him more of an outcast. I wanted him to have a family and my children were grown. I couldn't imagine it would be so – difficult – for all of them."

"You can't blame yourself for his childhood," I pleaded. "Marshall and Milo were close growing up. He had a family. It wasn't perfect but whose is?"

She patted my hand and smiled. "I want you to know how different they are at the core, you see. They look similar and sometimes share that similar stubborn streak, but their hearts are much different. We all have points of view based on our life experiences, dear. We like to think we make our own decisions independently – or maybe fate has a small role – but we are shaped by our history."

"What are you trying to tell me?"

"I'm trying to sprinkle a bit of wisdom around I suppose. I can't tell you what to do – just what I know after my many, many, many years on this planet."

We chuckled at her comment as Trish walked in with sweaty children. They jumped around the room going on about how they hoped Mrs. MacArthur stayed in hospital so they could play more. Such thoughtful kids.

On our way home, I asked Trish if she knew how Mrs. MacArthur and Milo were connected - that they were related. She gave me a side-eye and bit the inside of her cheek. I let her in on what I was told and promised not to push further. I could tell it wasn't intentional that no one had told me. It was assumed knowledge in the town. People were hurt, so it wasn't discussed.

What Mrs. MacArthur said bounced around in my brain. Wasn't the point of wisdom to learn from others' mistakes? If Warner Masterson could do it over again, would he have left his wife? Would he have married his wife at all if Milo's mother was the love of his life?

We all went into Trish's house together and put some kids' show on the television while she started lunch. She insisted she didn't need any help and was happy to cook for people in her home instead of a bar.

When she had something warming in the oven, Trish joined us in the living area. "What are you doing?" she asked me.

"I hope you don't mind. I saw this on the desk over there," I answered.

"No, not at all, but what are you doing."

I turned to a fresh page and met her gaze. "I'm writing a letter."

CHAPTER 40

Would this be considered the first letter I've written to you? It's a complicated issue, right? I've been writing to you for ten years but thinking you were Paul. I guess I didn't know Paul – especially because it was you – you see the issue here?

It's an understatement that this month has been insane. Is life-changing too dramatic? I think the no-drama ship has sailed, so I'll stick with that – life-changing.

A letter seems to be the best option right now and I'm kicking myself for not thinking of it earlier. Full transparency – I find you kind of irresistible. Not sure if you noticed that we never really have those all-night talks or you get off the phone first conversations. Do men even want that – or is it just to get a woman into bed? Maybe I missed that step and we can't go back.

You aren't much of a talker anyway. No offense.

Let's start with the overall deceptive tactics. I'm happy you came clean about being a part of Outreach Partners and the server crash before I found out from someone else. That's progress. I did find out about you owning our seed money corporation before you told me, so you would have been in deep shit if you hadn't confessed.

Not that you aren't in deep shit for, you know, the biggest lie of them all – who you really are.

I spoke with Mrs. MacArthur and I learned a bit about your mother. Parents always hope their children get the best of themselves. She sounded like a romantic, someone who loves deeply – like you.

Her face in our conversation showed me a lot of what I needed to know – she was regretful. She loves you, but it's painful for her. It gave me a small window of what it must have been like for you as a boy. How that must have shaped you as a man, wondering if you – just as you are – could be enough.

That's no excuse. You should have told me, but I'm starting to understand more about where your head was throughout this. How time flies by and before you know it, you're trying to dig your way out of quicksand.

I know you came to America for Mitch's funeral. I also know you weren't in a place to tell me who you were, but you wanted to be there for me. For someone who still remembers that day as being alone and ostracized, it means everything that you came. My memory will now include a man who loved me and crossed an ocean to try and protect me in any way he could.

I've come to realize that Paul seems to be an aftereffect of your actions. Maybe it's a brotherly competition or maybe he does have love for me, but it's too little too late. He left Claudia after I was here and he knew I had been with you. He moved to Winlin after you. He tried to stop you from coming to Maine all those years ago on a horrible day in my life when I needed support - because he couldn't come. Paul needs to be by himself for some time. I had six years and, looking back, I'm grateful for it.

People grow and change. In the past decade, I have grown with you. We have become who we are together. How many letters a year – 30 or so? You know the woman I am today. He caught up like binge-watching Netflix – it's not the same.

I will always have love for Paul, but I need that fresh start. I'm not sure if I can have it with you, but I'm willing to try. I'm willing to follow my heart for once.

I know you want to make up for lost time, but I want you to take a step back. I want to get to know you as you. I guess I'm asking you out on a date? Would you like to go to dinner – away from our home so I don't fall into your bed until I'm ready to fully trust us?

I have another request – call it a penance.

Switch homes with Trish.

We will still be close, but we can start a relationship like normal people. She's been a great friend and has said more than once she wishes she could be closer to me and Rita. It's only a few streets, so stop brooding about it (I can tell you are). You will also be closer to Paul and you two are brothers. Work it out.

This is a long-winded way of saying I want you, Milo. Everything in me says that we have a connection. I'm hurt by the things you did, but I have empathy for you too. I want to move forward – with you.

Don't ever lie to me again. If I look fat in something – tell me. If you don't like my parenting – say it. If you do anything that may cause me to run the other direction – confess.

I may slap you for calling me fat, scream that you have no idea how to parent, and I may leave, but don't ever lie to me again.

I do need you in my life, Milo. I'm following my heart. It takes a lot of courage and I'm scared, but I'm also incredibly happy as I write this.

I love you,

Mel

CHAPTER 41

"So how did it go with Paul? I want every gory detail," Rita demanded, as she brushed bronzer on my collar bones. We were in Robert's house in Cornwall sitting cross-legged on her floor. I was shocked he let any of us back in, but the house was full this weekend. He did have staff in the house and security at the door – lessons had been learned.

"It's not gory at all. It was sad, but he didn't seem surprised." I turned my head to see my makeup in the wall mirror. Rita always had a flare to make things a little extra bold, but I wanted that tonight. My bright red dress wouldn't do with a simple look.

"It was a four-hour talk," I continued. "I felt like I repeated myself a lot. He messaged Claudia while I was there to tell her I wouldn't have him, so that's something. I'm hoping she'll take that as a cease-fire."

"Fat chance," Trish said, walking into our room and plopping down on the bed. "You haven't seen the last of her. Is Paul still living in Winlin?"

"He is and he isn't," I answered. "A lot of the homes need

renovating and Milo and Paul have decided to work on them together. The one they just started is studded, so he's staying at the local Inn."

"I still find that weird," Rita commented.

"I insisted," I told her. "They are brothers and they are in business together. Men are wired differently. It's only been a couple of weeks, but it's already 'tolerable' is what Milo says."

"You left them together with a nail gun and means to cut up a body. You are a brave woman indeed," Trish added. "But I'm glad you pushed them to work together. They are family and time is going to make it better. Mrs. MacArthur was gushing the other day about how things felt right in the world."

"Well, not enough time has passed for Paul to be here this weekend. Sorry, but the house was destroyed enough last time without any testosterone involved," Rita said.

Robert had invited all the girls and their partners. He also extended the invite to the Masterson brothers, and all but Paul accepted. Robert met him at the pub for a drink before we left to make sure Paul was alright. The report we got back was that it was too soon, but hopefully one day we could be more of a family.

I felt a mix of relief and sadness. I have faith we can be together as a family – one day. He had filed for divorce with Claudia and already her list of demands ignoring any prenup was being battled by their attorneys.

She had dropped off Nina for a weekend visit over a week ago – she hadn't picked her back up – and her paperwork didn't ask for custody. Mrs. MacArthur jumped in to help and the kids were already getting along. I was glad that being a parent was below money on Claudia's priority list. Paul would still have Nina in his life.

"Beautiful," Rita commented and rose to her feet. I did love the look Rita had given me. I had a wing of eyeliner and a red lip. "They are doing fireworks tonight at the beach. Pretty sure it's illegal, but we can ask for forgiveness, not permission."

We followed her out of the room. I was the last to get ready. Lynn and her husband were sitting at the kitchen bar and shot us a huge smile when we walked in. She let out a whistle as we walked by and we gave a little strut and shake with giggles.

Robert opened the patio door with his elbow, carrying armfuls of champagne. Rita scurried to help him, joking that he didn't have near enough. They were paired so beautifully. She was still kind of brash and crazy, but Robert enjoyed her outspoken nature. He was taking Jack on golfing lessons starting next weekend and the kid had told me about it every hour on the hour since he found out.

Lynn and her husband held hands and popped off their barstools to go outside with the others. "You coming?" she bellowed, sashaying out of the door in her silver dress.

"We are," Milo said snaking an arm around my waist from behind me. I turned around and took his face in my hands. He had on a perfectly fitted suit and was clean-shaven with his hair combed back.

"You clean up nice," I gushed, giving him a light kiss.

"You are breathtaking, love," he said, cupping my ass and pulling me closer. We hadn't had sex in weeks since I gave him the letter.

I had knocked on his door not sure if he was even home. I handed him the letter and told him I was heading to Paul's house, but I would be back. The look on his face was devastation and my heart broke. I wrapped my arms around him, kissed him, and told him again that I was coming back. He started ripping open the letter as I jogged away.

When I got back, he was waiting on the porch with a huge smile and hydrangea flowers he had picked from the back garden. I joked that those weren't my favorite flower but they were my favorite color, so I would give him a pass. He told me he knew, and that's why he painted our front door blue. It made my heart soar. He knew me.

He asked me out on a date for a few days later. I asked why so far out and he informed me his girlfriend had volunteered him to move two homes and he wanted to get it done to make her happy.

"Could we just skip dinner and head straight for bed?" he asked with fire in his eyes.

"Naughty and NO," I remarked. "This is a special night for Rita. She needs my support pretending she doesn't know Robert is about to pop the question."

Milo laughed and pulled me closer kissing me again. "This might be a special night for Max too you know."

I tilted my head and gave him a quizzical look. He took my face and turned it to see Milo's brother Maxwell. He was on the patio talking to Trish. He had a huge smile plastered on his face and she had his full attention.

"Oh my God, do you think really!" I gasped. "That would be so amazing."

"We wouldn't want them to go too fast though," he quipped. "That never turns out well."

I grabbed Milo's hand and gave him a playful yank towards the door. From the steps, I could see the beautiful dinner table on the level below. Twinkle lights surrounded a white and pink table. Gold and white plates were stacked with folded napkins and seating cards. The center of the table had cut roses laid from one end to the other.

"How gorgeous," I whispered to myself.

"Mel!" Robert hollered from the head of the table. "It's customary for the last to the table to give a speech."

This part of the night had been rehearsed. I would give a speech distracting Rita so he could get the ring and some courage to propose. Milo wrapped his arm around me as we approached the table and took his seat still holding my hand. I grabbed a glass and swallowed the lump in my throat.

I would just like to say how wonderful it is that we are all here together tonight. In our busy lives, we find time for each other, and that's special. What's remarkable though – what's the thing that makes my heart full – is that we all found each other so we had this opportunity to be together. It's not easy to find good friends – even less so to keep them and make time for them. And love, well, that can be a disaster under the best of circumstances. Through some miracle, we entered each other's lives and we made it to this beautiful evening. I won't take a second of it for granted. I won't waste any time not following my heart. I want to tell you all now, how much I love you. Every day I pray for your happiness and that you find joy in this world. I hope I can be a small part of that in any way I can. Cheers!

Everyone applauded and one by one rose to their feet to clink glasses. I turned to Milo. "Cheers," I said.

"Hearts and stars," he replied, and I giggled. "I love you Carmela – have for some time now you know."

I couldn't reply before he took me in a passionate kiss. I jolted when I felt cold champagne spill down my arm and then I saw Rita jumping up and down in the corner screaming Yes.

"Someday soon that will be us, you know," Milo said, nipping at my neck.

"I know, and I love you too, Milo," I gushed, holding him tighter. "I've loved you for some time now too."

The End

Epilogue

1 year later

Milo would be home any minute and I was pacing. Our home was still a construction zone so I felt more like I was playing frogger than steadily walking around the house. Two months ago, he had moved in and started knocking out the wall between the duplex. The only thing that didn't have drywall dust on it was Eva's room, which was kept pristine. In a few weeks, we would be in Cornwall for Rita's wedding and he was pushing to get it done by that date.

I spun the large rock on my left hand. Milo had proposed the night he moved in, hiding the ring in a box of coffee supplies he knew I would tear into like a Christmas present. *He's going to be upset.*

I thought back to the past weekend. The Saturday night before I knew everything would be changed forever. My heart fluttered remembering Milo coming home crazy with lust. He had slammed the door behind him and made his way over to me in three strides. He carried me to the bedroom and ravaged my body all night long. I think I might have blacked out at one point from the most intense orgasm of my life. At two in the morning, he woke me again with his face between my thighs wanting more.

I heard Milo's key in the door and my pulse quickened as he stepped inside. "Hello love, I brought us some dinner. Why don't you pick out some wine?"

My heart sank. This wasn't going to be easy. I grabbed a bottle of red that I knew Milo liked and brought it to the table. "How was your day?"

"It was as good as it could be. Paul's divorce still isn't final."

I turned the corkscrew and huffed. "That's not a surprise. What does that mean for Meghan?" Paul had started dating a wonderful woman named Meghan last month. I met her briefly but heard all about her from Milo. She didn't want to date Paul until the divorce was final but she was conveniently at the Winlin Wag every time he was. Sometimes it felt like everyone in this town was ready for this divorce to be over.

We had made strides towards being a family, but I knew Paul needed to find his someone to close that chapter of our lives. From the sounds of it, Meghan was that someone. She wouldn't wait forever.

My hands were shaking as I set the table. Milo's brow furrowed. "What's wrong?"

I made a trip back to the kitchen and grabbed a shoebox and set it down on the table. "Sit down babe. You'll need to be sitting for what I'm about to tell you."

"You are scaring me," he whispered, taking a seat.

"Okay, well, I'm kind of scared," I admitted. Milo grabbed my hand and gave me a soft kiss. He brought my palm to his thigh and waited. "I think we may have to change our plans this year."

My throat went dry and I struggled to continue.

"Is this about going to Cornwall with Trish and Max? The house will be done I promise, and Eva and Jack will have fun. The first family trip is a big deal – I get it."

I shook my head still unable to process my thoughts. I pushed the shoebox over to him. He took it in his hands and shook the box with a grin.

"I-I'm talking about the trip to Maine. I-In June. We won't be able to go."

Milo flicked the top of the lid off with a sideways grin. When he registered what he was looking at his smile stretched across his entire face. His broad shoulders shook with laughter and I could see the flush in his cheeks.

"Are you serious?" he choked out.

"I'm sorry. I'm on the pill. I haven't been perfect lately with the move and the construction and Rita's wedding and oh my God the new project at work. I tried to catch up on them which I KNOW is dumb, but I thought it would be okay."

Milo interrupted my rambling with a strong passionate kiss. When I broke free, my breath was ragged. "Milo – do you understand what's happening?"

"Yes, love. I'm going to be a dad. This is the best day of my life. I didn't think life could get any better but wow - this is better."

"So, you are okay? You aren't upset? I messed up the pill. This is my fault."

Milo grabbed me and brought me into his lap. He stroked my

cheek with his hand and kissed me again. "I'm not upset one bit. I'm thrilled. Call Trish – Call Rita – Call Mrs. MacArthur. Is it too soon to shout this out to the world?"

"I don't know the rules, Milo. I think we should start with Eva. We need to let her know she's going to be a big sister."

Milo's smile grew wider if that was even possible. "Could we tell her the paperwork is in for the adoption too?" Milo had filed to adopt Eva shortly after he proposed. He had great attorneys with his companies that had fast-tracked everything. All we had to do was sign after the wedding and it was official. Eva wanted to change her name to Eva Morgan Bennett, keeping her biological father's name, but honoring the man that would raise her for most of her life.

"We could just put up a banner across the house. Then all of Winlin would know," I quipped. Milo's eyes flickered.

"That was a joke, Milo!" I shouted, pushing on his shoulder.

"Mel, are you happy?" Milo asked rubbing his hand up and down my back.

My eyes watered as I looked at him. I had never been happier in my entire life. Even with a ripped apart house, work stress, wedding stress, and constant nausea - I was beaming with joy.

"I am, Milo. I love you. I've loved you for some time now in fact."

With that, Milo lifted us both from the chair and started towards the bedroom. "The food will get cold," I protested.

"All that matters is this moment," Milo responded. "Let me show you how much I love you."

"Insatiable," I gasped.

"Forever," he responded and shut the door behind us.

ABOUT THE AUTHOR

Adeline Hamble is a wife, mother, and animal lover. You can find her binge reading love stories and writing in her spare time. *Keep in Touch* is her first novel with many more to come. For notice of coming books please email adelinehambleauthor@gmail.com.